THE BIG
DECAY

The Big Decay

Copyright © 2024 by Eric Willliford

All rights reserved.

https://thedefpix.com/

Book Cover by Def Pix Entertainment

Editing: Geraldine N. and Teresa F.
Beta Reader: Paola Llerenas
Print edition ISBN: 979-8-9889373-2-6
E-book edition ISBN: 979-8-9889373-1-9

WARNING; This book features graphic depictions of sex, violence, and themes of suicide.

You have been warned.

Dedicated to everyone that's been on this
crazy journey with me.

IYKYK

Also by Eric Williford

The Dead Ate Cheese

THE BIG
DECAY

Table of Contents

ANORA

My mom would say today
is the worst day of her life.
Until tomorrow.

And the red and blue lights that bleed through the windows of the cabin act as my timer. At any moment, they'll kick the door in and haul my black ass out in cuffs. Until then, my fingers punch word after word into my laptop's keyboard. When my imagination fires on all cylinders like this, it's tough for my digits to keep pace. But they do the best they can.

Another page complete.

Toni Morrison once said, "Write the book you want to read." After you cut your veins and bleed all over the blank page, why go back and live through those experiences? Will the urge hit me to revisit all this awfulness? Doubt it. But never say never.

Another page complete.

Even if this book is the death of me, it wouldn't be so bad to put these things onto the page. Maybe even turn these three hundred and forty-seven pages into something worth reading. Or hell, turn it into a movie. There may not be enough here for a series. Maybe one of those limited series.

Another page complete. Three hundred and forty-eight pages.

In music, they say your first album is the one you spend your entire life working on. When your first novel sets the literary world ablaze, the expectations for your follow-up can be crippling. How do you write something in two years that will outdo something you spent twenty-seven years creating?

Three hundred and forty-nine pages.

None of this matters to my agent. All he wants is something he can sell. Quality be damned. Besides, he has to shoulder some of the blame for all this. But he's an optimist. He wouldn't shoulder the blame. He'd share in the credit. Sales people. What can you do?

Three hundred and fifty pages.

"Come out with your hands up."

They're getting antsy. Are there news crews out there? The last thing this situation needs is a bunch of uniformed hayseeds putting on a show for the cameras. Parading some educated black chick out in handcuffs for all the world to see. Look at your delicate genius now. It was never my intention to be a martyr. Or a criminal.

Three hundred and fifty-one pages.

"I repeat, come out with your hands up."

The bigger question is, will they shoot me the moment the door opens? Do they know that in certain circles, the name Canna Wendle carries some weight? Not enough to get me out of this mess, but could it be enough to get me a fair trial? Is there such a thing for someone who looks like me?

"We have the means to tear your door down. We don't want to, but we will."

Anora's gaze burns a hole through my skull. She can be quite unsupportive. "It's almost done, Anora. Be patient."

The End.

Six letters. One period. The first draft is complete.

Three hundred and fifty-two pages.

This is a first draft written under duress. No time to worry about the spelling and grammatical errors. Or the pacing. Or the line edit. Or the copy edit. My gut tells me it needs to lose about twenty to twenty-five pages. Hemingway said all first drafts are shit. This is no exception.

Time to send this thing to my agent. One quick email with the manuscript attached. He'll know what to do. My publisher has a stable of qualified editors who can take this and turn it into something respectable.

"We're going to count to ten, then we're coming in."

Damn. This email is gonna have to be short. No time to explain what happened to his precious cabin.

"One."

No time to take down all these damn notecards.

"Two."

No time to explain how things went so terribly wrong.

"Three."

No time to explain how Anora came into my life.

"Four."

No time to explain why this manuscript is such a mess.

"Five."

No time to explain why my name is all over the news.

"Six."

No time to explain which of the things they're saying about me are true.

"Seven."

The email is done. Complete with the attachment and a carbon copy to my alternate email. Just in case.

"Eight."

Send

One word. Four letters. Guess he'll read the manuscript and form his own opinions. Fingers crossed; they can turn this slop into the masterpiece expected from me.

"Nine."

"Alright, on my way. Gimme a minute to get dressed."

My mom would say any
fool who buys a mattress
deserves to get ripped off.

Before

And the alarm goes off at seven-fourteen in the morning. My closet is of modest size, so it's no problem for me to stretch my limbs. When you sleep in the fetal position, your legs and back can become stiff. Early morning stretching has been a mainstay of my daily routine.

The door opens and shoes litter the floor of the bedroom. To clear out enough room to sleep, they had to get tossed out of the closet.

Boots. Flats. Tennis shoes. Sandals. They all find their way back into the closet. Nothing gets the early morning blood flowing like organizing your shoes as you put them back where they belong.

And the restaurant is half empty on a Friday night. The staff and owners are too hip to notice.

The Boyfriend insisted he take me out somewhere nice. Somewhere trendy. My red dress and black Chuck Taylor kicks let him know this chick can clean up well. But she ain't changing for anybody.

"You mind?" says The Boyfriend.

His fork hovers over the last piece of what was a decadent slice of chocolate cake. The sleeve of his designer suit hovers over the chocolate frosting. Amazing how dessert can have someone throw all caution to the wind.

"All you."

He demolishes the last bit of cake and savors each bite.

"You don't have to rub it in," I say.

"Sorry, you want to get another?"

"One's plenty."

The Boyfriend says, "Is it though?"

The pinot gris is a tad sweet for my taste, but it sliced through the butteriness of the shrimp scampi. The Boyfriend stares at me as the glass lowers from my lips. I ask, "Is there cake on my face?"

"You look stunning."

On instinct, my hand searches for a strand of hair to brush off my forehead. The Boyfriend's smile is delicate and boyish. The floppy blonde hair and the piercing blue eyes help. His skin is perfectly tanned from his four-mile jogging route through the city.

"I mean it. You should wear dresses more often."

"Then it wouldn't be special when I do."

"This is a special occasion?"

"It's our anniversary. Five months."

The Boyfriend shifts his weight from right to left, the way he always does when he gets embarrassed. "Didn't know people celebrated such a thing."

"Some do. I saw it on a blog or something."

He says, "You didn't get me a gift, did you?"

"Thought I'd dress nice for the occasion."

The Boyfriend can't keep his eyes off my breasts. "I can't wait to unwrap you."

"Easy there, Romeo."

"You should use this in one of your books."

My eyes dart around the restaurant. "Use what?"

"This conversation. It's good stuff. What do you writers call it? Banter?"

The laugh bursts out of me. My hand moves to my mouth to suppress it. "You wanna get a tea or something? Coffee?"

"Still no pages, huh?"

The last drops of wine coat my tongue. "A place like this has to have chamomile, right?"

The Boyfriend says, "My cousin, he writes music. When he's struggling, he looks to other art forms for inspiration."

My eyes scan the restaurant. Desperate for a server. "Green tea. I should do a green tea."

"He'll check out an art gallery, or a film. He's always searching for inspiration."

Are all the servers on break at the same time? Are they having a team meeting? "When combined, caffeine and L-theanine can improve brain function. Green tea has both."

"Are you not interested in hearing about my cousin?"

"I'm trying to improve my brain function."

The Boyfriend says, "There's an art gallery a few blocks from here. Let's stop in. See if it sparks anything in you."

"First, I get a green tea."

And the painting features a pink circle in the corner of a black canvas. Minimalism defined. As we stare at it, my full attention is on the scent wafting through the air. A potent mix of biscuits and hot dogs. Odd for a place with so much snobbery.

The Boyfriend rubs his chin. "I wonder what people have to go through to make truly great art."

"Usually some type of psychological damage. Or, they watch a shit ton of movies and TV shows. Read a bunch of books."

Some guy in all black with an extra-long blue beard arrives with a tray full of pigs in blankets. Guess we have an explanation for the smell. The Boyfriend grabs two. Offers me one.

"No thank you," I say. "You wanna unwrap this gift?"

My mom would say you should never trust someone who gets paid by percentage.

And my agent is the perfect mix of Yale white guy literary intellectual and used car salesman. He's exactly what an author should look for. An education that can get him into the room, and enough of a two-bit hustler to close the deal.

He scooped me up after reading my short story in Lamplight. He was direct, plain, and matter-of-fact. He reminded me of my mother. His office is exactly what you'd expect it to be after meeting him for three minutes. He probably keeps a swimsuit calendar in his desk drawer under a copy of *Atlas Shrugged*.

"They're breathing down my back, Canna," the agent says. "It's a good thing. Sort of. I'd rather they weren't breathing down my back."

The agent has more paper clips than anyone should ever need. It's the digital age. How much paper is this guy printing? Could be this office has some sort of paper clip-based hierarchical system. Is there someone with more paper clips than this guy? Where does he rank?

The agent continues. "But it would be worse if they didn't care. At least they seem to give a shit. Are you listening to me?" He points to the animal in front of me. The one arranged out of paperclips. "What is that?"

"It's a horse." But upon closer examination, it occurs to me, "Or maybe a dog."

He sits back and sighs. "Cards on the table. You are not a bestselling author. A bestselling author can play the whole eccentric genius card. A bestselling author can wait for inspiration."

"The word inspiration never crossed my lips."

"You are what we call a selling author. Critical darling? Sure. But numbers don't lie. This industry is full of hacks who wrote one novel and faded into oblivion. Gone." He leans in the way he does when he wants me to pay attention. "They didn't strike while the iron was hot. For whatever reason, it took them too long to follow up their breakthrough with another title. Everyone forgot about them. The world kept on spinning."

"And they were punished by being shot into space?"

"Start producing pages before you get dropped."

I say, "They'll drop me? This quick?"

The agent dives into his desk drawer and pulls out a set of keys. He slides them across the desk. "I've got a cabin by a lake. It's secluded. Beautiful. Quiet. No distractions. Take your typewriter, laptop, or whatever you use, and hunker down. Get me some pages so I can hold them off."

And The Boyfriend blocks my path to the dresser. "You could be gone for weeks. Or months. Shouldn't we have discussed this?"

With my eyes on him and a no-look toss of blue floral panties into a suitcase, I say, "By discuss, you mean asked permission?"

"I meant the actual definition of discuss."

I say, "There's nothing to discuss because as soon as he offered, I accepted. The only discussion is me telling you I'm going. Which is what I'm doing now."

The Boyfriend takes a seat on the edge of the bed. "I'm not trying to control you. I thought we were at a place where... I don't know."

He slides over and my butt hits the bed next to him. With his hand in mine, I say, "This isn't about you. I'm not trying to interrupt what we're doing. Got it? But please, don't make this an either-or type thing, because this is my passion."

The Boyfriend smiles. "Can you at least have conjugal visits?"

There are times when he makes it difficult not to kiss him.

My mom would say some towns only have six hundred people for a reason.

And my car makes its way through downtown Briar Springs. A town with one three-screen movie theater and four diners. It's the epitome of small-town America. In a Jim Crow sort of way.

Before long, my eyes are taking in the lush greenery on either side of the two-lane highway. Birds bask in the early morning sun as they rest their wings and let the breeze do the work. An occasional car or truck roars by on the opposite side of the road.

The two-story cottage sits two hundred feet from the lake. There's a shed in the back. Woods surround the property.

Inside, the atmosphere is cozy and sophisticated. The few things that aren't wood are leather. An area rug covers much of the floor. It's perfect for someone with a closet full of flannel.

The bedroom is of a modest size, with a closet and a dresser and a bed and a nightstand. Some clothes get hung up, some get folded and stuffed into the dresser.

The hardest part of writing are those first few words. At the kitchen table with my laptop open, nothing comes to me. What is this thing even going to be about? Who are the characters? What do they want? Does this thing require an outline?

Into the phone, I say, "I wanted to let you know I made it to your cabin. This place is amazing. Thank you so much. I'm feeling good. Got my laptop out. Pages are on their way. You're gonna love it. Okay. I gotta get back to work. Thanks again!" The last word escapes my mouth milliseconds before the recording cuts off.

Back at my dreaded laptop, my fingers type. The four letters pour out of me. Repeated over and over again until they fill the page.

blahblahblahblahblahblahblahblahblahblahblahblah

My finger mashes the delete button until it's all gone. Seconds later my keys are in hand and this chick is out the door.

And the pizza parlor is a family joint with a small bar. Only a handful of patrons sit and eat greasy pizza. At the bar with my face hidden behind the six-page menu, the choices are overwhelming. What is a breakfast pizza? Who eats eggs on pizza?

The bartender makes his way over. His arrogance arrives seconds before the rest of him does. Every bit the backup high school quarterback whose dad thought he should be starting. "You decide yet?"

The menu gets lowered to reveal my face. "I'll have the large Margherita to go."

"A large? I hope you have someone to help you eat it." He grins. He's charmed himself more than me.

"I like leftovers."

"I'll have it out to you in fifteen minutes."

"Can I get a glass of pinot gris while I wait?"

"I wouldn't recommend the wine. It's pretty cheap. We got some good —"

"I prefer cheap wine. Keeps me humble."

"Let me get this in and I'll pour you a glass."

There's a family in the back corner. Dad has a smear of dirt across his forehead. Mom is dressed to make sure she doesn't attract attention from a would-be rival male. It's unclear how long their greasy lipped freckled toddler has been staring at me. A smile should show him the requisite amount of civility. It doesn't. He continues to stare. The bartender arrives with an empty glass and a bottle of cheap white wine.

I say, "That kid is freaking me out."

The bartender pours the wine. "He doesn't know any better. The closest most people in this town get to seeing someone like you is Sportscenter."

"That doesn't make it any better."

"Don't worry. These are good people. Even if their kids are strange." He extends his hand and tells me his name.

As I accept his invitation to shake, "I'm Canna. Nice to meet you."

"You staying in town?"

"I am."

"A little vacation, huh? How long you in town for?"

"Depends on how long it takes me to finish my book."

He takes a step back. Crosses his arms. "Ohhhh. A famous author."

The wine is so terrible it's damn near charming. It's what you get when you order wine in a place like this. As I lower the glass from my lips, I say, "You know why they put tomatoes, mozzarella, and basil on a Margherita pizza?"

"Because it's delicious."

"True. But it also represents the colors of the Italian flag."

The bartender smirks as if he's solved a puzzle. "I see you're into Jeopardy-type stuff. This town has a lot of history and cool facts you'd be into." He pulls out a pen, grabs a napkin, and scribbles his number onto it. "Maybe while you're in town, I can volunteer my services as a tour guide."

"I have a boyfriend."

"You're free. But I'll have to charge him extra."

With napkin in hand, I say, "Not sure I can trust a guy with two first names."

The bartender says, "You seem like a lady who enjoys a little danger."

And the area around the cabin is pitch black. Clouds diffuse the trickle of light the moon offers. A noise in the darkness brings me to an abrupt stop. My hands tighten around the sides of the enormous pizza box. My entire body is on alert.

Another noise. This one is from the side of the house. Is it the trash cans? "Hello?"

No answer.

Something scrapes along the side of the metal trash cans. My eyes have adjusted to the darkness. There doesn't seem to be anyone or anything over there.

The scraping persists. My feet remain rooted in place. "I can hear you." Still no answer. Left foot first. Then the right. Two steps closer to the door and a crashing sound shatters the silence. The top of the trash can falls off and clangs against the side of the can as it hits the ground.

A certain calmness hangs in the air. My gaze fixates on the trash can and its discarded lid. Inside the trash can, something moves against paper. Or plastic. Out of the top of the trashcan, a pair of yellow eyes stare back at me. "Hello there."

In the pantry is a can of corn that gets poured into a bowl that gets placed next to the trash cans. "You deserve better than trash, my little raccoon friend."

The pizza is cold. Can't blame the pizza parlor, or the bartender. It was a ten-minute drive home; the raccoon ordeal was another eight minutes. Sure, there's the option to reheat it, but this chick is hungry now.

My second book gets a title: *A Certain Calmness*

My mom would say
butterflies are beautiful
because they have a
liquid diet.

And the blank page stares back at me as the hot ginger tea makes its way down my throat. The morning sun against my skin isn't enough to make me forget about the lack of progress.

When the phone rings, it's a welcome distraction. The words on the screen say it's my agent. He asks if I've settled in. He asks if I've got any pages done. I tell him I'm having a flood of creativity. I tell him this is exactly what I needed. I tell him I've even got a title for the book. He calls me a genius and tells me to get back to work.

Another sip of tea. The day grows hotter by the minute. Soon the tea is gone, and the page remains blank. When the phone rings again, the screen says it's The Boyfriend. He tells me he misses me. He asks if I miss him. I tell him yes.

I tell him the work is flowing out of me. I tell him the book has a title. I tell him the title. I tell him I had pizza for dinner. I tell him I've made a friend. He says that was fast. I tell him my friend is a raccoon. He tells me to make sure my new friend doesn't have rabies.

When we hang up, the page is still blank.

And *Ethiopia's Shadow In America* marches from my earbuds into my ears. The hike through the woods is serene. A butterfly makes its journey from one blooming flower to another. It takes to the sky. Off to find a comfortable place to die. Something putrid hits my nostrils. My body gags. But curiosity gets the best of me.

The smell pulls me into a clearing and a rusted Chevy Tahoe comes into view. Against the rear passenger side door is the body of a man dressed in cowboy boots, jeans a size too small, and a bolo tie. On the ground next to him is a revolver. Judging by the blood on the door and the hole in the back of his head, he fed himself a bullet.

My first instinct is to call the police, or the sheriff, or whatever passes for law enforcement around here. But something thirty yards away catches my attention. The black man's body is intact. the back of his head has a gaping hole. Skull and brain fragments cover the ground and the other body.

The other body nearly costs me my tea and breakfast. The face is an abstract piece of art constructed of broken bones, dried blood, broken skin, and broken cartilage. Where the nose should be, there is flattened skin. Where the teeth once were, there are exposed gums.

And it's back through the woods. My pace is quick. Whatever happened back there, it's none of my business. Somebody will find those bodies and that someone can call the cops. Or the sheriff. Or whoever.

But.

And now my earbuds are in my pocket, and the phone is against my ear. The dispatch lady is asking me questions. My forearm attempts to shield my nose from the odor. More questions. More half-baked answers. Dispatch lady isn't a fan of me.

The phone gets hung up when the dispatch lady finally agrees to send the sheriff. With the phone in one hand, and out of the corner of my eye, I see her. She's in the backseat of the Chevy Tahoe. Her hair is an electric blue bob. She's dressed in red tracksuit pants and a white t-shirt. She's barefoot and filthy. Cute and innocent. She's also a doll. An inanimate object. Roughly the size of a Cabbage Patch Kid. Her eyes meet mine as I pull her out of the Tahoe.

And the deputy examines the body of the cowboy who blew his own brains out next to the Tahoe. "This fella here looks like the one we got that APB on a few weeks back."

The sheriff makes his way around the SUV. His face is grizzled from years of sun damage and disposable razors. "You'll have to be a bit more specific."

The deputy says, "Pretty sure it had something to do with the institution about an hour west of here."

The sheriff makes his way over. His eyes shift from me to the doll in my arms and back to me. "You're saying you just stumbled upon this here scene?"

"I was out for a hike."

The sheriff says, "With the doll?"

"Oh, yeah. I was hoping to get some fresh air. Get the creative juices flowing. I'm a writer."

The deputy makes his way over to the other bodies. His hand hovers over his holster as he goes.

The sheriff keeps his attention on the doll in my arms. "We don't get many people like you around here."

"Writers?"

"I'm talkin' about urban folks."

I say the only thing I can say. "Wow. Okay then."

The sheriff finally looks me in the eye. "Never told me about the doll."

"Not sure what there is to tell."

"You can start by telling me why you bring it with you on your walks."

"I use her to bounce ideas."

"You talk to it?"

"When I have ideas."

The deputy doubles over once he gets a good look at the carnage. He gags as he says, "Sheriff, looks like this colored fella bashed this other fella's head in with a rock."

The sheriff glances over at his deputy. Turns back to me with a face full of disappointment. "Friend of yours?"

"Surprisingly, we don't all know each other," I say. "As much fun as this is, I've done my civic duty, right?"

The sheriff scribbles something into his notebook. "You're free to go. But stay available in case we need to contact you."

My mom would say
nightmares are the only
time we're truly alive.

And the page remains blank. The doll sits on the kitchen counter. She watches me stare at the blank screen on my laptop. She watches me make a pot of spaghetti. She watches me make garlic bread. She watches me drink an entire bottle of Pinot Gris. She watches me eat dinner. She watches me clean the dishes. Her eyes observe the fraudulent chick as she fails to put words onto the page.

The doll sits on the edge of the couch, always watching. Judging as the fraudulent chick opens another bottle of wine. Midway through the second bottle and still no words. No inciting incident. No beginning. No characters. No story. No plot.

And now the fraudulent chick lays in bed, unable to sleep. Drunk off wine and failure. Another day. Another blank page. Nothing left to do but laugh.

Hours pass. The fraudulent chick stares at the ceiling. She tries screaming into her pillow. When it feels like it's a hundred degrees, she takes off her clothes. When the room spins, she closes her eyes.

But sleep never comes. Only the questions fill her head. What if my legacy is the one book? What if another book never comes out of me? What if my agent drops me? Or my publisher? Is it so bad if one book is all I'm known for? A flash in the pan. A one-hit wonder who gets exposed as a fraud. The literary equivalent of Fyre Festival.

There's more to me than one book. There's another story inside of me. It's a matter of finding it. Giving it life. Putting words onto the page.

Before long, shoes are out of the closet. The fraudulent chick lies on the floor of the closet in the fetal position. Eyes squeezed shut until they aren't. Even the closet has failed me.

And it's morning, and the fraudulent chick is hungover and tired. The doll watches as two eggs get scrambled and two pieces of bread become nearly burnt toast. A little extra butter to soften them and some cinnamon to brighten my mood. The ginger tea soothes my nerves, my throat, and my stomach.

The doll lies on the table across from me. She watches my every move. She knows the fraudulent chick should write instead of nursing a hangover. I say to the doll, "You got a name, or should I call you doll?"

Now the fraudulent chick has resorted to speaking with inanimate objects. If this isn't rock bottom, there's no such thing.

Wait. What's happening? My first instinct is to run, but something keeps me glued to the chair. Eyes on the doll. I ask, "How did you do that?"

Now on my feet. My mind races. Is it the lack of sleep? The hangover? Or has imposter syndrome wormed its way into my psyche. My frustrations have boiled over into madness. But she repeats herself. I ask her, "Your name's Anora?" Seated in the chair with my eyes glued to the doll, I say, "I dig it."

Another sip of tea. Having someone to talk to isn't so bad. "Things haven't been going great for me, Anora. It's been four years since my book came out. Everyone wants to know what's next. Truth is, maybe there isn't a next." For whatever reason this makes me laugh.

The fork shovels the last of the eggs into my mouth. It gets chased with another sip of tea. "Are you saying the answer is to have adventures like Ernest Hemingway?"

Another bite of toast. Another sip of tea. "I've never been to a place like that, Anora. What would I even wear?"

My mom would say
sex is the only true
performance art.

And the neon sign on the front of the building reads *Southern Comfort*. Despite being dressed in my only pair of heels, my best jeans, and my sexiest top, this bouncer guy remains surly.

He says, "We're not hiring."

"It's okay. I'm here to have a drink and check out the girls." The wink lets him know this isn't my first rodeo. Even though it totally is.

"By yourself?"

"Is that not allowed?"

The bouncer studies me. Lingers on my breasts longer than necessary. Finally, he says, "ID."

The speakers can hardly contain the shrieks of some eighties rock song. If a mobile home grew up and became a strip club, it'd be this place.

My eyes and brain try to take it all in at once. The half-naked strippers. The guys stuffing money into their crotches. The girl on stage doing the full splits while naked. A red-haired girl in the back is bent over some guy's lap. Her head moves up and down.

There's a table in the front. Right by the stage. I assume it's like a sporting event with the most expensive seats in front. It seems to be first come first serve, so sure, why not?

It's not long before a waitress makes her way over. This is my first time in a place like this, but my gut tells me she's about nine years too old for this job. She takes a moment to size me up before she says, "It's a two-drink minimum."

"I'll go with a pinot gris." My smile reassures her I am, in fact, harmless.

She says, "Do you know where you are?"

"Is it okay to order a vodka soda?"

With an epic sigh, she saunters off.

Across the room, a stripper removes her pink thong and lays across the laps of three guys. All of them dressed in dirty work boots and filthy jeans. They shower her with dollar bills. One guy's middle finger vanishes inside her. It's a lot to process.

A green-haired stripper sashays to my table. Her hair matches her fern-colored bikini. She takes a seat at my table and smirks. "The girls can't stop talking about the chick who ordered a pinot gris. Figured I'd come see for myself."

"This town could use a wine distributor."

She laughs and tells me her name.

My hand searches for a strand of hair to brush off my forehead. "I'm Canna."

She smirks. "Maiden voyage?"

On the stage, one of her co-workers starts her dance. With a dollar bill in my hand, I say, "No. I'm what you call a connoisseur of the ladies."

The yawn assures me she's not buying it. For emphasis, she snatches the dollar out of my hand, saunters to the stage, and crams it down her co-worker's thong. She returns to my table, takes a seat, leans back, and folds her arms.

I say, "Okay, this might be my first time."

"It's obvious."

The moody waitress returns and places my vodka soda on the table. "Ten bucks."

My hands dig through my purse until they find the cash. "Money goes quick around here, doesn't it?" The waitress grabs the money and marches off to give attitude to another table.

The drink is more water than anything else, but it's a good thing because this vodka was most likely propping up the bottom shelf.

My green-haired friend sucks her teeth at me. "You're not gonna offer to buy me a drink?"

"Is that the custom?"

"You can get a lap dance instead."

"Thank you, but I have a boyfriend. He's not around, but you know. I'm taken."

"It's a lap dance, sweety. Neither one of us will get pregnant."

"What's something like that cost?"

"Thirty bucks. One song. Fifty bucks. Two songs."

"Pass."

My green-haired friend stands to leave.

"Wait, I thought we were hanging out?"

She says, "You're funny."

"I'll buy you a drink as soon as the alcohol lady comes back."

Her eyes scan the area. On the hunt for new prey. When she decides there is none, she returns to her seat. "Why are you here?"

If she knew a doll told me to get dressed and come in here, she'd run away. As strange as it may sound, her company puts me at ease. "I'm hunting for inspiration. Like Ernest Hemingway." Another sip of my watered-down drink. "This place is like its own little world. I love it."

The stripper studies me as my lips suck on the straw. Did telling her this is a field trip make things awkward? As if she's some nearly extinct species and my aim is to study her in her natural habitat. Sometimes my mouth needs to stay shut.

My green-haired friend says, "I bet you read a lot of Anne Sexton, don't you?"

Three emotions cycle through me. The first is shock. The second is admiration. The third is, "Thirty bucks? One song?"

And my green-haired friend leads me into a chair in the back corner behind a black curtain. She takes the money out of my hand and puts it in her little jade purse. A new song takes over.

Her opening move is to turn around and grind her butt into my crotch. It's not as awkward as it should be. Her hips shift in unison with the beat. She leans back and her shoulders lay across my breasts. With her head on my shoulders, her hair cascades down my body.

Indole is an aromatic, heterocyclic, organic compound. It's the reason jasmine smells the way it does. It's the reason my green-haired friend is so intoxicating. It's one reason she can do whatever she wants with me. Her scent fills my nose and spirit.

She slithers off me as the song crescendos. Now on her feet, she turns to face me. She brings her face inches from mine. Our eyes lock. Her hands search my body. She drags them over my hips and along my rib cage. She brings them across my breasts. A gasp escapes me. Her eyes never leave mine as her fingers graze my nipples.

My mouth is dry. My body is relaxed and ready. For what, it's unclear. But she needn't say more than a word. Whatever she wants, we can do it. Let them watch. She leans into my ear as the song ends. "If you're ever looking for more inspiration, I make house calls."

My mom would say the only writers worth a damn are the ones who write instruction manuals.

And Anora watches me from the dresser. The words tumble out of my mouth with a complete disregard for the toothbrush. "I can't believe I have never been to a strip club. I met this stripper. She had green hair. You'd get along with her, Anora. She's smart. And confident. Whatever she's got, if she bottled it and sold it, this chick would be first in line."

Now dressed in my favorite oversized sleep shirt I slip into bed. "It's hard to tell at the moment if my little excursion will help with getting some words onto the page, but damn. It was worth it if only for the fun. Is my green-haired friend off work yet?"

Sleep comes easy.

And when my eyes open the next morning, they see the front door. Panic sets in. When did I leave the bedroom? Where is my sleep shirt? Why am I naked? Off the couch and on my feet. "Hello?"

No answer.

In the kitchen, all the cabinets are open. Even the fridge is open. The chairs are on top of the kitchen table. The faucet is on.

Everything gets closed and turned off. None of the windows are open. No signs of forced entry. But just in case, I grab the biggest knife in the butcher block. " I have a knife."

Silence.

Until the phone rings. It scares me. It rings again. It's nowhere to be seen. Another ring. Is it coming from the couch?

The phone is between the couch cushions. It's The Boyfriend. Now is not the time. He gets banished to voicemail. This chick has a mystery to solve. Also, she needs to get dressed.

The bathroom is empty. No signs of weirdness.

The bedroom seems in order. Anora sits on the dresser. Right where she was last night.

Next thing I know, laughter explodes out of me. It doesn't stop. The knife falls to the ground. The laugh consumes me to the point of cramps. My naked body doubles over. Tears streak my face.

And the kitchen is back in order. Yours truly has on clothes. Anora sits on the kitchen counter. Notecards cover the kitchen table. With a mouth full of cold pizza, the ideas come fast and furious. Inspiration at last.

It could have been the strip club. It could have been my green-haired friend. The outline comes together like an assembly line. Grab card. Scribble a scene description onto it. Put it in the pile. Bite the cold pizza. Sip the warm tea. Grab another notecard. Repeat until the ideas vanish.

The pizza box is so large, the only way to get it into the metal trash can is to bend it. With my hands on either side of the table-sized box, and my knee in the middle of it, my raccoon friend's empty food bowl catches my attention.

Anora watches as the bowl gets refilled with a new can of corn. "I'm hungry, and I've earned a break." The empty can gets tossed in the trash under the sink. "I'm not sure how I would keep something like that from The Boyfriend." With my raccoon friend's bowl of corn in my hand, I say, "True. It's only dinner."

The bartender is on the other side of the phone. He remembers me from my order. He's polite. Charming. I tell him the reason I'm calling. He says he's free for dinner. I give him the address of the cabin. He says he's looking forward to it.

Anora watches me change out of the sweats and t-shirt and into something more suitable for a shopping trip. "The ship has sailed Anora. I hope you're right about this." A quick glance in the mirror. "I know we haven't spent a lot of time together. But I'm starving and there's no food here."

Anora sits on the couch, facing the front door. With keys in hand, I say, "The bartender is coming over tonight, like you suggested. Tomorrow we'll hang out. I promise."

My mom would say the world went to shit after humans stopped bartering and started using currency.

And this diner is one wolf painting away from being a full-blown flea market. Junk crowds each crevice. A vintage upright piano sits by the door. It's listed for three hundred bucks. By the kitchen stands a five-foot wood carving of a black bear with a tray in its hands. Five-hundred bucks.

Ordering food would be great, but not a single person has come by to drop off a menu. The door opens and in struts a young white couple. Both are dressed for a hike. They pass the piano and the woman smiles as she leads her male companion to a seat by the window. Their asses hit the cracked plastic benches and the server with the high and tight bun gallops over with two menus. She places them on the table and takes their drink orders.

As high and tight rushes to fill the order, we lock eyes. I say, "Excuse me. Could I get a menu?"

Hair Bun brushes past me as she makes her way towards the bear. "Yeah."

She drops the menu on my table and delivers two glasses of water to the young hikers.

The menu has all the staples. Flapjacks, not pancakes. Real pork sausage, not the turkey stuff. American waffles, not Belgian. This place is so red, white, and blue they don't even serve French toast.

Hair Bun and her favorite table talk about me. It's obvious because they divert their eyes the moment my menu lowers.

Never mind them. This chick needs food, and there's a full day in front of me. Will it be the blueberry flapjacks or the cheese grits?

And the bookstore smells of yellowed pages. Guaranteed, there's a first edition of Uncle Tom's Cabin bracing a table in the back. My hands grasp a copy of *Eating The Inferno*. Even after four years, there's still nothing like holding a copy of your own book in a bookstore.

At the register, the cashier with the rhinestone scorpion brooch rings up a stack of notecards and the book. I tell her I like her brooch.

"Thank you." Scorpion Brooch eyes the book. "You gonna be reading this?"

"Sort of. It's for a friend." By her reaction, Scorpion Brooch has no clue what it means. It's not my most obtuse statement ever, but it's pretty close. "Why, have you read it?"

Scorpion Brooch snickers. "I have."

I say, "Would you recommend it?"

"That'll be ninety-three dollars and fifty-eight cents."

There's an ungodly number of notecards.

Scorpion Brooch takes the credit card from me and says, "I would. But it's not for the faint of heart. This isn't gonna ruin anything—"

She notices the name on the credit card. Glances at me. Digs through the bag, past about eighty dollars' worth of notecards, and pulls out the book. Her eyes dance from the book to the credit card, and back again. "This is your book?"

"It is."

"I'm impressed."

"I appreciate you reading it."

"The fact you survived having a mother like that and now," she studies me, "look at you."

"That which doesn't kill you, or so they say."

Scorpion Brooch stares at me long enough for it to get awkward. Finally, she says, "Wish I had my copy here for you to sign."

"You can keep this one." Before the words are out of my mouth, the pen in my hand has already spelled my first name inside the cover.

"You are too kind."

As my last name nears completion, I say, "Happy to do it. You can still charge me for the book." Scorpion Brooch grabs the book and stares at the signature then takes off her rhinestone scorpion and offers it to me. "For you."

"Oh, I couldn't. Thank you, though."

"It's okay. My mother gave it to me."

"Now I really can't accept it."

Scorpion Brooch chuckles. "My mother has given me a brooch three times a year since I was ten. One on my birthday, one on Christmas, and one on Easter. I have a hundred and thirty-five of these things. Turtles. Swans. Flowers. Please. I insist."

She pushes the brooch into my hand. I say, "That's a lot of brooches."

"It is."

"Thank you."

The cashier, with a signed copy of my book in her hand, says, "Mothers, they mean well. After all, us women need to stick together."

Not even nine steps out of the bookstore and there he is. The deputy. He leans against his squad car until he maneuvers over to block my path. "Hey, miss—"

"Were you waiting for me?"

"I was." The deputy shifts his eyes to the ground. "It's not official police business." His gaze shifts, but he can't look me in the eye. "I don't mean that in a creepy way. Look. I… well, I wanted to apologize for what I said the other day."

It's hard to tell if he already gave the apology, or if there is an actual apology on the way.

"When I used the word, *colored*."

"I remember."

The deputy finally looks me in the eye and says, "I shouldn't have said it. It's not right. It slipped out is all. And well, I apologize. I promise you, I'm gonna keep trying."

I say, "Trying is all any of us can do."

And the grocery store is exactly what you'd expect in a town with only one grocery store. A phone call interrupts my hunt for steaks. It's The Boyfriend. He can wait.

At the register, the check-out chick stares at me as she blows a huge pink bubble. It's unclear if this is a territorial thing or a flirting thing. She doesn't scan my items until after the bubble pops.

Bubble Gum says, "You're the chick stayin' at that cabin by the lake, aren't you?"

"Guilty."

Bubble Gum snatches the box of condoms. Sighs as she runs them over the scanner. "Coming out here to fuck a bartender don't make you special."

It's settled. The bubble blowing was a territorial thing. The only question left is, "You're not gonna overcharge me, are you?"

Bubble Gum says, "I'm sure you think you're hot shit. But you're not."

"I don't think I'm hot shit."

"Good. Because I've fucked him six times." Bubble Gum points to another cashier three registers away. This one with too many piercings. "See that chick over there? She's fucked him eleven times. Between the two of us, that's—"

"Seventeen times. Got it."

Bubble Gum has one brown eye and one gray eye and they both hurl insults at me. "You swear you're cute, don't you?"

I say, "For what it's worth, I won't return his calls after I'm done with him."

My mom would say even
bees steal honey from
other hives.

And putting the groceries away gives me a great excuse
to pace under the watchful eye of Anora. The train
has left the tracks, there's no going back. "I sure hope
you're right about this, Anora."

The steak finds a home in the refrigerator.

"You were right about the strip club trip. It stirred
something in me. Look at all these notecards."

Anora stares at me.

"Word travels quick around here. No doubt the bartender told the entire town."

The cabernet finds a home in the back corner of the
counter.

"You should have seen the chick in the grocery store. Not sure what it says about me if I go through with this. I mean, he banged the girl at the register six times. Is this guy the notch my belt needs?"

The mushrooms find a home in the refrigerator.

And the hot water from the shower does nothing to ease my trepidation.

Anora watches as the crazy girl wrapped in the towel gives herself a pep talk.

"There's no reason for the two of them to meet, right? Sure, The Boyfriend wants to come visit, but he won't appear without an invitation. It's only a matter of telling him my work is going too well for interruptions. Problem solved."

The black lacey thong with the matching bra are on the bed. "You're right. I need to broaden my worldview if I'm going to tell stories."

The towel comes off and I grab the undergarments. "Got an opinion, Anora? Too much? The goal is to appear interested, but not desperate."

In the mirror, the bra looks good held against my tits. "Doesn't matter. By the time we get to this point, it's game on."

And we start with the crispness of the Sauvignon Blanc. The cab can wait until the steaks. Two bottles of wine should be enough for me to go through with this madness.

The bartender raises his glass and smirks. "To new friends."

Ugh. He needs to call up his "A" game, quick.

We each take a sip. The seasoned steaks sit on the countertop next to my phone. He says, "Letting the steaks get to room temp before tossing them on the grill. Pro move. I'm impressed."

My eye roll is a natural reaction. There's no stopping it.

He notices and tries to recover. "I'm not impressed because you're a woman. I'm impressed because most people don't know how to cook a decent steak. Male or female."

"When you put it like that, thank you."

Mr. Impressed takes in the cabin. "I gotta say, hearing from you was a bit of a shock."

"I bet."

"You were pretty upfront about your marital status."

Another sip of wine to let his comment hang in the air. "Is that what we're calling it?"

Mr. Impressed says, "Taken. Available. You know."

"I'm far from married."

"Only a boyfriend?"

My glass finds its way to the counter. "This conversation isn't conducive to what you're hoping to achieve."

The vacant look in his eyes suggests he doesn't know what *conducive* means. I say, "Tell you what. I'm going to put these on the grill. When I come back, have a new topic ready to go."

The charcoal grill is nice and hot. Desperate for red meat. The steaks sizzle as they hit the grate. Mr. Impressed better like his steak medium rare because it's what he's getting. With any luck, he'll turn this thing around and close the deal. This chick has a book to write, and this dude isn't helping.

Back in the kitchen, Mr. Impressed refills our glasses. "Tell me about this book you're writing."

"It's nothing like my first book. Which is good. I guess. Nobody wants to be a one-trick pony."

Mr. Impressed takes a sip of his wine. "What if the one trick is amazing?"

"Even the greatest trick of all time gets old if it's repeated too often."

The sound of bees buzzing fills the kitchen. Both of us turn to the source.

My phone.

Before his smirk turns into a statement, the phone is in my hand. A quick push of a button and the bees no longer buzz.

Mr. Impressed leans against the counter. "Boyfriend?"

The rest of my wine gets demolished and the bottle refills my now empty glass. "You want a refill?"

He extends his glass. "Too bad this isn't red wine. I hear it goes great with chocolate."

"You can't be serious with that line."

He licks his lips. "I'm serious."

My full-body gag is the only answer I can muster. He straightens his posture. Guzzles his wine, wipes his lips and says, "I assumed, you know..."

"No. I don't know."

He takes another gulp of his wine. "Can't you take a joke?"

"Is that what I am to you? Some sort of chocolate fetish?"

He tries to take another gulp of wine, but his glass is empty. "I'm nervous. Sorry. Forget I said anything."

"Tell me something. Is black chick on the same row as Asian chick on your bingo card?

He grabs the bottle. "You're overreacting. I was making a joke." He shakes the bottle. Yep. It's empty too.

"It's best you leave."

Finally, he turns to face me. "What? No. We haven't even eaten yet."

I grab the empty bottle and say, "You can buy something on your way home."

He crosses his arms against his chest. "You called me over. If you weren't interested, you shouldn't have dialed my number."

The empty bottle is light in my right hand. In my left hand is my glass of wine. "You never would have gotten a call had I known you were a giant douche."

"Let's have some more wine and eat those steaks. Forget all about this." He closes the space between us.

"No longer interested."

He tries to wrap his arms around me, but a quick step back puts me out of range.

Undeterred, he takes another step towards me. His eyes are full of determination. He snarls. "We both want this."

"You need to leave. I don't know how much clearer I need to be." A sidestep to get around him so he can't corner me. He grabs my arm and gropes my ass.

As he leans in for a kiss, he says, "This is about your boyfriend, isn't it? He called and now you're having second thoughts. You're all full of guilt, aren't you?"

Now in his grasp, I'm pulled towards him like a tractor beam. "I changed my mind because, turns out, you're gross."

His breath is humid. The Sauvignon Blanc stings my nostrils. Our noses are an inch apart. "I don't mind being your fetish. And you can be mine."

In my left hand is my empty glass. He leans in for a kiss. My left forearm meets his chest. With all my strength, my left arm extends and pushes him back. This gives me a little space to work with.

My right hand still clutches the empty wine bottle. In one swift movement, the bottle gets flipped and now my hand grips it around the neck.

It's all in slow motion. His eyes fixate on the bottle. Unsure if this chick has the balls to do what he assumes she's gonna do. My eyes fixate on the side of his head that's about to get cracked open. I swing. He's too shocked to duck. Guess you could say he takes it like a man.

The bottle explodes against the side of his face. Blood and glass rain onto the floor. Now only the jagged remains of the bottle are in my hand.

He staggers and uses his hand to check the side of his face.

Yep.

It's blood.

Lots of it.

He gathers himself and lunges for me. "Bitch."

Instinct takes over. A quick sidestep and his initial attack misses. He's off balance. The blood has blurred his vision. What's left of the wine bottle is still in my hand. A quick thrust and the jagged edge pierces the left side of his neck.

Another jab. This one puts a hole in his jugular. Blood pours out of both wounds. He teeters and clutches his throat.

I watch as he collapses.

Mr. Impressed attempts to stem the flow of blood. But it's no use. It covers his hands. Seeps onto the surrounding floor. The pool grows bigger as the seconds pass.

What's left of the bottle slips from my hand and shatters against the floor.

His arrogant eyes grow cloudy. A cough and blood splatters onto the cabinets under the sink. His breath becomes desperate. More vacant. There's an attempt to speak, but he only manages a few gurgling sounds. One hand remains at his throat. The other hand reaches out for me.

Even in death, this dude is trying to get laid.

My mom would say you haven't lived until you tried to sleep in a prison cell.

And the duct tape around the bartender's neck has slowed the blood flow. The gardening gloves keep my hands stain-free. Pulling out his cell phone takes some work, but my nimble fingers accomplish the goal. Despite the gloves.

With an arm looped under each of his shoulders, dragging this dude across the floor is no easy task. My lower back burns from the strain. He leaves a trail of blood across the floor as we trawl from room to room.

His blue pickup truck sits behind my car. His rusted-out Chevy is about 5 years older than me. The bartender hits the ground next to it. A quick stretch to loosen my back. Finally, some relief.

The trail of blood leads out of the cabin and right to the truck. Keys to the truck are in his left pocket.

Lowering the tailgate to the truck is the easy part. The hard part is getting this two-hundred-pound rapist lifted and into the bed. My first plan is to sit in the truck's bed, lean over the edge, and hoist him in.

This proves too difficult.

Now on the ground and straddling the rapist, it occurs to me how much he'd enjoy this. My arms go under his shoulder so we're chest to chest. His blood covers my shirt and seeps into my "get lucky" bra.

The struggle is real. After a few attempts, the top of his back is flush against the tailgate. With my body to his side, but my arms still looped around his chest, it's easier to lift him into the bed of the truck. Once his head is in, it's only a matter of pushing the rest of his body inside.

In the shed, there's a tarp and a stack of bricks.

The bartender's body gets covered with the tarp. Six bricks along the edge of the tarp will hold it in place.

And now the entire cabin reeks of bleach and household cleaners. To Anora, the entire thing is hilarious. At least one of us is having a good time.

A gloved hand submerges the brush into a bucket full of bloodied water. "I don't have a choice. It's not like I can bury the whole truck."

And in the comfort of a warm shower, the blood washes off me.

The dirt washes off me.

The murder of the rapist washes off me.

The only thing that doesn't wash off is the thought of nearly getting raped. I assume it will haunt my dreams until my dying day.

And now dressed in jeans, a t-shirt, and a baseball cap, I put Anora onto the bed and say, "I'll be back in the morning."

As soon as the truck roars to life, *Pop That Pussy* by *2 Live Crew* explodes out of the speakers. The realization that I nearly fucked this guy forces me to choke down a tinge of vomit.

And the truck rumbles along a two-lane road. It's a little after midnight and the moon supplies the only light. The truck is old, in a pre-power steering sort of way. Deep turns require two hands and gritted teeth. But after a while, the truck submitted and accepted Canna Wendle as its new queen.

The plan is simple. Ditch the truck somewhere far away and random. Hop on a bus back to that shit hole town, pack my stuff, and get the hell out of dodge.

Like the bartender didn't try to rape me.

Like this chick didn't kill a man with a bottle of wine.

According to Anora, some new life experiences would help me with my book. Be like Hemingway, she urged. Get out of my shell. See things. Hear things. Taste things. Could be she knows what she's talking about. Is it smart to even include this in my book?

There's a pop. The truck shakes. The handling gets worse. This could only mean one thing.

A flat tire. Fuck.

It takes both hands to get the truck onto the shoulder of the two-lane country road. The headlights are my only source of light. On the front passenger side, there's a hole the size of a golf ball in the tire.

In the bed of the truck, it's hard to maneuver without touching the dead rapist. All the tools are in the back corner. The jack. Lug wrench. Spare tire.

Finding the frame on these old trucks is a simple task. Thirty seconds later, the jack has the truck off the ground enough for me to swap out these lug nuts.

As each nut comes off, it gets placed in the spare tire for safekeeping. Once the flat tire is off, it gets tossed onto the bed of the truck. The rapist won't mind the company.

Fumbling around in the dark, my foot kicks the spare tire. The lug nuts clang into each other as they're tossed out of the wheel.

"Damn it."

Now on my knees, my hands search the dirt for the lug nuts. They could have rolled anywhere.

Car lights approach. My attention stays on the dirt until the lights pull in right behind the truck.

The sound of a heavy metal door is followed by a gravelly-voiced stranger who says, "Need some help?"

It's close to 2 AM, and this chick is on her knees in the dirt. At this point in the night, my instincts kick in. First, grab the lug wrench. Second, get onto my feet and face whatever comes, head-on.

In the blackness, it's hard to make him out. But he continues toward me. The closer he gets, the more of him comes into view. He's heavy-set with a beard. A flannel shirt. About sixty years old.

Flannel Shirt says, "Got a flat?"

"I got it. Thanks though."

He closes in. "Young woman out here by herself. Not too safe."

My grip tightens around the lug wrench. "I know."

Flannel Shirt stops only a few feet away from me. Surveys the area. "Saw you on all fours. You lose something?"

An honest answer could give him enough information to kill me or help me. But he doesn't even wait for an answer.

"Got a daughter about your age. Taught her how to change a flat as soon as she got her license. Your old man teach you?"

"Mom."

Flannel Shirt says, "Good on her."

Something in the way he mentioned his daughter makes me ease my grip on the lug wrench. "I lost the lug nuts. They're around here somewhere."

A glance at the other tires and he says, "Wanna know a trick?"

"If it helps me get back on the road, I'm all ears."

"Take one lug nut off each of the other tires. It's not ideal, but it'll get you back on the road."

After a brief sigh, "Brilliant."

"When you're around long enough, you learn a few things." Flannel Shirt takes a step towards the back of the truck.

He can't see what's in the truck bed. One body is enough for tonight. I block his path and say, "I'll get that back one. Do you mind checking over there to see if you can find the ones I lost?"

"My eyes aren't what they used to be."

I say, "The hope is, you'll find something I overlooked."

"Guess it's worth a try."

Flannel Shirt kneels and rummages around in the grass. It's not long before both of the lug nuts are off the two back tires. Seconds later, the third lug nut is off.

We work together to attach the spare using the three lug nuts. My new friend helps me gather the tools when we're done. He grabs the jack. "I'll toss these back in the truck for you."

"Thanks."

Flannel Shirt takes two steps towards the back of the truck when it hits me. "I'll get it."

Before he can protest, the tools are in my hands and the back of the truck is only two feet away. I smile and say, "You've been so kind. I've got it from here. I don't want to hold you up."

Flannel Shirt says, "Pretty self-sufficient, aren't ya?"

"I try."

My new friend hooks his thumbs into his belt loops. "First chance you get, stop and get a real tire. Avoid high speeds so you don't get another blowout."

"Thanks for your help. Can I give you some money or something?"

My new friend waves off my generosity. "Take care of yourself now, okay." He saunters back to his car, gets in, and drives off.

And the truck limps through the city streets as dawn announces a new day. There's a parking garage attached to a mall. It's ten minutes after six and there's nobody in sight. It's perfect.

The spare tire makes the truck even more of a bear to turn. Inside the garage, there isn't a single vehicle. A space by the entrance won't do. Neither will a space close to the mall. Too many cameras. Something in the middle will be perfect.

My baseball cap hangs low. Barely over my eyes. After a brief inspection to make sure there's nothing to incriminate me, it's time to get out.

The morning air hits my face. A welcomed relief after a night of stress and murder. With any luck, it'll be days before anyone notices the truck.

The city streets are empty. There's nobody to see me toss the gloves, the keys, and the bartender's phone into the sewer.

If you've ever been to a bus station at the crack of dawn, you know the type of folks who hang out there. In another time, these folks would be perfect fodder for a book. One look and it's clear these people have done more than existed. These folks have lived.

The seats aren't comfortable, but exhaustion washes over me. The bus hasn't even made it out of the city and this chick is fast asleep. My eyes pop open at the first stop out of the city.

It's only a guess, but it seems like this place is about ten miles outside of town. If anyone comes looking for me, best not to get off the bus in the same area as the cabin.

The walk takes the better part of the day. It's warm, and the sweat comes thick and heavy. Walking along the two-lane road would bring too much attention to me. Instead, my path is through the woods along the highway.

And the blisters on my feet are so bad the only thing left to do is collapse onto the floor of the cabin. An hour later, my eyes open. My mouth is as dry as a powder house. It takes three glasses of water to quench this thirst.

In the bedroom, Anora stares at me from the bed. "Sorry. Took longer than I thought."

I pull the suitcase out of the closet and say, "What does it look like I'm doing? We gotta get the hell outta here." In my arms are clothes ripped from hangers. "Someone is going to find the truck with the body in it. I shouldn't be here when they do." The clothes get crammed into the suitcase.

"You expect me to sit here like I didn't murder a guy in the kitchen?" My undergarments get stuffed into the suit-case. "There's going to be questions either way, Anora."

In the bathroom, I gather my toiletries and say, "You believe being here to answer them is the best idea?"

She makes a good point. Skipping town now would make me look suspicious. Also, there's a book in need of writing. But the idea of sticking around makes me uneasy. Especially after my first run-in with the sheriff. He would love nothing more than to haul my ass into the station and give me a mugshot.

"It's scary how persuasive you can be, Anora." Time to reverse course. First things out of my suitcase are the undergarments. "First sign they're onto me. We're getting out of here."

With my hands full of bras and socks, I say, "Nobody knows he was coming over. Who would I even tell?" My favorite quarter-cut socks are halfway into the drawer when the realization hits.

"Oh shit."

My mom would say the
jealousy of others is the
measure of your success.

And Bubble Gum stares at the pack of condoms in her
hand. "You want to return these?"

I say, "He never came over."

She echoes, "He never came over?"

"This transaction will run a lot smoother if you stop
repeating everything I say."

Between obnoxious smacks of her gum, she says, "You
got a receipt?"

"No. But you remember me."

"You can't return items without a receipt."

The line grows to five customers. It bothers me more
than it does her. "It's not like they're used. The box isn't

even open. Can't you give me my money and put them back on the shelf?"

"Can't do it, hot stuff."

"Get someone who can."

Bubble Gum blows a bubble. This one is more petite than her usual bubbles. After it pops, she says, "They're only like five bucks."

"Five bucks I want back."

Bubble Gum rolls her eyes and smacks her gum as she leans into the microphone next to the register. "I need a manager to register four."

Her disdain for me is palpable, but it doesn't matter. My goal isn't to slow down the line. The strategy is to make this entire fiasco memorable so if the sheriff comes knocking, all these shoppers will remember these unopened condoms and the angry black chick who wanted her money back.

For a little icing on the cake, I ask, "Were you with him?"

Between smacks of her gum, she replies, "Maybe."

"You're exhausting, you know that?"

Bubble Gum relishes this. A quick glance at the condoms and back at me with a grin plastered all over her face. "Somebody jealous?"

"Not hardly."

A burned-out and miserable manager guy arrives. A discolored smudge from two washes ago stains his tie. After a phlegmy cough, he asks, "What is it?"

Bubble Gum never takes her eyes off me. Nor does she lose the grin. "Lady here says she wants to return these condoms. She ain't got her receipt."

The phlegmy manager arrived ten seconds ago and already wants out of the situation. Or maybe he wants out of life. He squeezes in behind the register. "Store credit is the best we can do."

Fine. Mission complete and it's time to get out of this place and away from Bubble Gum. I say, "She never mentioned the store credit. If she had, I would have taken that and saved you the trouble."

Three blocks west of the grocery store sits a costume shop. Who knows what compelled me to go inside, but it was a fantastic decision. Each square foot is crammed with bizarre costumes.

Need one of those two-person horse costumes? They got it.

Are you the proud owner of triple D breasts you want to show off while dressed as a beekeeper? They got you covered.

Nestled in the back corner of the shop are various wigs of all shapes, sizes, and colors. Next to them, a beaded partition separates the costume shop from a secret room.

Forty minutes later and the guy at the register with the rip-van winkle beard eyes my selections. He rings up the blue wig with the flowing locks and the red tracksuit pants.

I can't help but ask, "What's behind the beads?"

"Porn."

"Oh. Wasn't expecting that answer in a place like this."

"Forty percent of our revenue comes in October." He brandishes the wig and tracksuit pants. "That's this stuff. The other sixty percent comes from butt plugs and ball gags."

My mom would say the best sex she ever had was in the institution.

And my purchases intrigue Anora. As I cut the wig into a bob, I say, "Wait until you see the pants."

When it's done, we both admire my work. Not to toot my horn, but the wig is a perfect bob. A spitting image of Anora's hair. I smirk and say, "Look at us. A couple of chicks living life on our own terms."

And the moment my green-haired friend arrives on stage, her eyes take me in. Right in front. There's no need for us to smile. We let our eyes carry out the conversation for us. Despite the crowd, her focus is on me, and mine on her.

Her bikini top comes off. My eyes linger on her breasts. Her eyes say the dance is for me.

She crawls across the stage. My throat dries. A sip of my vodka soda helps, but only for a moment before she lies back and spreads her legs.

My little black dress is strapless, so it looks best without a bra. Her gaze lingers on my erect nipples.

Her mint-colored bottoms slide past her ankles and float to the stage. My eyes tell her we should talk when she's done. She shifts to the edge of the stage to give me a better view. A twenty-dollar bill leaves my hand and drifts until it lands next to her.

The dance ends. She collects her money and mint-colored bikini. My green-haired friend inches her way to the edge of the stage and sucks her lower lip into her mouth. In an instant, the goddess is on her feet. Still gloriously naked.

She leans in close; her lips are centimeters away from my ear. Her bare breasts rest on my chest. My dress is 95 percent polyester and 5 percent spandex. It's the only thing separating her pink nipples from my caramel nipples.

My green-haired friend smells of vanilla and it takes all my self-control to not lick her. In my ear, she asks, "What can I do for you, gorgeous?"

The thrill of her closeness and the sound of her voice sends a wave of lust pulsing through me. My right leg moves to cross over the top of my left leg. My green-haired friend senses my leg as it rises and she uses the outside of her right hand to force it back down and keep my legs open. A heeled foot rises and comes over my leg.

She asks me a question but my mouth won't form an answer. With my leg between hers, she lowers herself onto me. Her wetness leaves a trail as she pulls herself along my leg until our bodies converge.

Some asshole in the back whistles.

We have the attention of the entire club. Time stands still. Her body squeezes against me. Her breasts press against mine.

Whistles rain in from all over the club. A crumbled dollar bill hits me in the back of the head.

My green-haired friend says, "You know how much they'll pay to watch us fuck, right here, right now."

With her trail of wetness on my leg, and my panties sopping wet, I finally whisper, "What time do you get off?"

My green-haired friend grinds herself on my leg and moans, "I'm getting off right now."

My mom would say if you're going to fuck a man, take more than one at a time to cover your bases.

A nd in the bathroom, dressed in only a blue thong, my reflection receives a pep talk. "They accused Oscar Wilde of sodomy. Hunter S. Thompson consumed whatever drug he could get his hands on. Amiri Baraka wrote *The Autobiography* while serving time in a Harlem halfway house. Louisa May Alcott had an opium addiction."

Goose pimples populate my body as my hand pushes the door open. The bedroom is dark. Moonlight seeps through the blinds. There she is. Sprawled out on my bed. Naked. Eyes closed as she slides two fingers in and out of herself. My green-haired friend pinches her nipple and asks, "What took you so long?"

I say, "Are we all square?"

She raises her hips off of the bed and moans. "Let's not talk about money."

Next to her left leg is the white t-shirt, red tracksuit pants, and the blue wig. My green-haired friend uses her foot to point to the perfect little pile. "You want me to wear this?"

"Yes please."

Her eyes close as she brings herself closer to climax. "First, take the thong off."

The wet mark comes into view when the thong is around my ankles.

She pulls her fingers out, slides her body to the edge of the bed, and gets dressed. Her eyes take in my pussy as she grabs the tracksuit pants. A quick hop to pull up the pants. The bounce of her breasts makes my mouth water.

The white t-shirt gets slipped over her head and she grabs the wig. She adjusts it so the ensemble is in order. A quick pull on the shirt. A tug on the wig. A yank to the pants, and Anora stands before me.

My blue-haired friend closes the space between us. She slides her hand around my waist and pulls me in close. "Have you been fantasizing about this?"

"I have."

Her tongue is in my mouth, and her hands run over my body. I give in to her. Time slips in and out. One minute, our tongues dance inside our mouths. My blue-haired lover kneels in front of me at the edge of the bed. Only the blue wig is visible between my thighs as her tongue presses against my clit.

She rises up and we're face to face. We work together to get her out of the costume.

Seconds later, only the blue wig remains. I'm on my stomach and she uses her tongue to chart a trail from the top of my ass and up my spine. Her breasts rest on my back as she sucks on my earlobe. She slides a hand under me and cups my breast. When she pinches my nipple I tell her, "Do whatever you want with me."

Two of her fingers fill my pussy. My hips drive up and down in response to the fucking. When my hips hit the sheets, they dampen some more. Between moans, I say, "Sit on my face. Now."

My blue-haired lover does as she's told. She flips me over and rides my face. She gasps for air and says, "Have you ever squirted?"

I pull my tongue out of her, tilt my head to the side, and say, "Once. But it took two guys."

"Challenge accepted." She flattens herself against me and buries her face between my legs. My blue-haired lover rolls me over so we're on our sides. Her nose settles between my pussy and asshole. Her tongue is everywhere at once.

The moans pour out of me. She tastes sweet and smells of vanilla. The warmth of her thighs relaxes me. My arm pulls her leg back to open her more.

She does the same to me. The air rushes up my thigh. Her saliva mixes with my cum and it glistens my leg. A finger teases my asshole.

In response, my finger teases her asshole. Her body tenses and her hips coerce my finger into her ass.

My blue-haired lover's thumb glides along my thigh. She's lubricating it. Confirmation comes when she slides it into my ass. A jolt shoots through me. The ecstasy comes in waves. My toes curl.

Her moans grow louder and my finger responds with circular motions in her ass.

She palms my butt with her free hand. Her thumb drives in and out of my asshole.

My tongue drags across her shaven pussy. She explodes all over my face. Neither of us has any control left. Pleasure builds inside me. It could happen at any moment. The waves intensify. Her thumb presses against the inside of my ass. Two fingers drive in and out of my pussy. They slide along my engorged clit. All I can say is, "Oh fuck. Don't stop."

She doesn't.

Muscles seize as my body explodes. The stream covers her. My face burrows between her legs. There's no air, only the scent of vanilla and her sweat. There's no way for me to see how much came out of me. Judging by the way the sheets cling to my legs, it was a lot.

My blue-haired lover says, "That a girl."

We disengage. The wig looks like it fell in a lake. The object of my lust pulls it off and tosses it to the floor. Her body glistens as she slithers along my warm skin until she lies next to me. The wet spot is so big we're both in it. We're so spent, neither of us cares.

And in the shower, the warm water pelts my back and loosens my tense muscles. The goddess who did this to me is on her knees. She washes the inside of my thighs and legs. Water pools in her palm. She cups my pussy with it. Her attention to detail makes me weak in the knees. She says, "You only paid for an hour."

The water soothes me. With my eyes closed, I ask, "How long has it been?"

"Turn around."

Now the water massages my face. Her nipples dig into my back. She leans in and says, "I lost track ninety minutes ago."

Her body is no longer against mine. Where'd she go? I turn around for answers and once again the water massages my back. The words topple out of my mouth. "I can give you some more money." She has her back to me. Her hands are on the tile as she inches her legs apart.

Facing the wall, she says, "You can work it off."

Her back arches and her ass sticks out towards me. It's an invitation.

And the cold night air sails in through the open door. The air floats between the towel and my nakedness.

My green-haired lover takes a step out and turns to face me. "You know what intrigues me about you?"

"I'm the only chick in a fifty-mile radius who knows who Anne Sexton is?"

A smirk. "You're not nearly as innocent as you let on." She turns and makes her way across the yard to her immaculate silver Jeep.

I laugh and say, "I'll buy some toys. For next time."

She doesn't even turn. "Sounds fun."

The devil on my shoulder wants me to drop the towel and give her one last look. The angel on my other shoulder says let her go.

My green-haired lover turns to me with her hand on the door. "All your future sessions are on the house."

The angel wins and the towel stays on.

My green-haired lover hops into her Jeep and drives off.

The bedroom smells of sex and it's better than fresh-baked cookies. The towel falls to the floor, and my naked ass heads straight for the closet. My hands can't open the door fast enough. Inside, Anora sits on the floor. I scoop her into my arms and say, "Could you hear us?" With Anora tight against my chest, we collapse onto the damp sheets.

She rests between my breasts as I stroke her hair. "Next time, I'll arrange it so you can watch."

My mom would say queen ants do whatever it takes to survive, even if it destroys the colony.

And tiny feet crawl along my lips and cheek. A peaceful slumber ends and panic sets in. The morning sun blinds me as my eyes open and take in the area.

My face is in the dirt.

The tiny feet on my lips and cheek belong to a regiment of ants.

On my feet in an instant. To the side of me sits a pile of cartilage and tiny bones. Blood, dirt, and fur cover my naked body.

Wait. Fur?

Whose blood is this?

Fur?

A quick exam for cuts or gashes turns up nothing.

Whose blood is this?

The muscles in my stomach clench and my body doubles over. A couple of coughs and whatever is in there now sits at the top of my throat, ready to make its escape.

Two fingers go into my mouth, pincher style. The bile rushes up, but it subsides before the apex of my mouth. My fingers clasp onto something. As my fingers pull it out, something brushes against my tongue. It's long and the fur tickles the back of my throat.

My eyes go wide as the tail comes out of my mouth. Both hands work to pull this thing out of me.

But it keeps coming out.

How long is this thing?

Finally, it's out of me and on the ground. The tail is covered in blood, bile, and god knows what else.

Did that come out of me?

Acid hangs in the air, stinging my nostrils. My body heaves and vomit spews out of me. It splatters onto the ground and the liquid shrapnel peppers my exposed ankles and feet.

A moment to catch my breath. Still doubled over, my eyes stare into the sick that poured out of me.

Is that? No. It can't be.

Scattered amongst the fur, entrails, blood, and organs are little bits of corn.

Oh fuck.

Two bare feet carry me back to the cabin. Branches and limbs scrape and scratch my exposed skin. My pace quickens. This is the dolls' doing. The little blue-haired bitch is jealous.

How can she be mad when the whole thing was for her? The clothes. The wig. This was my gift to her. She must know this.

Pain surges through my left foot. There's a cut on the side, below the pinky toe. Must have been a twig. No time to worry about it now. No more games. If the doll has something she wants to say, she can say it to my face. The little bitch, so clever with her games. Let's see how she enjoys getting the stuffing ripped out of her.

The cabin comes into view. To the side of my car sits another car. An older model hatchback with a donut tire in the back.

What now?

Four steps into the front yard and they come into view. Bubble Gum and Too Many Piercings. At the front door with their backs to me.

They must have heard my footsteps because Bubble Gum turns and glares at me. She barks, "Your lover boy missed his last three shifts at the — Is that your blood?"

"What's it got to do with me?"

Too Many Piercings sports a face full of repulsion. "Fuck that shit. Why is she naked?"

I stop a few feet from them and say, "You were the last one with him. Whatever happened to him happened before he was supposed to see me."

Too Many Piercings can't take her eyes off me. "This bitch is into some voodoo shit."

Bubble Gum smacks on the wad of gum in her mouth. "Is that his blood?"

"What? No. I hit a deer and had to bury it."

They both look at my car. Bubble Gum says, "I don't see no dents."

This chick and her double negatives. Makes my skin crawl.

The detective with all the piercings folds her arms and delivers a mouthful of sass. "I don't see no shovel."

A quick cross of my own arms and I snap, "Maybe I should ask the questions? Like why are you sneaking around my property?"

Bubble Gum says, "We weren't sneaking. We rang the doorbell."

Too Many Piercings says, "But you were busy with your naked ass voodoo shit."

"I want the two of you gone. Now."

Bubble Gum says, "You're hiding something."

"I'm hiding something? Didn't you say you were with him the night he flaked on me? How about I call the sheriff? Tell him what you told me."

Bubble Gum takes a step towards me. "Whole town knows he was coming over to fuck you. And now the whole town knows he's missing."

She's proud of herself. The smug smile. Too Many Piercings arrives beside her to co-sign whatever comes out of her mouth.

Too Many Piercings says, "You still ain't told us why you're bare ass naked."

Her colleague adds, "Don't need to be naked to bury no deer."

"I've had enough of both of you and all your double negatives. You need to get off my property before I call the sheriff."

Too Many Piercings sucks her teeth.

Bubble Gum blows a giant bubble.

The fury rises inside me. My hands form a fist. Part of me wants a fight, even though they outnumber me. They may win, but they'll know they were in a scrap. "You don't want me to call the sheriff. I can look at you and tell you've got some priors."

That landed. If the crazy naked chick covered in blood is ready to call the sheriff, what else is she willing to do?

Too Many Piercings says, "Let's go. We don't want any part of her voodoo shit. Probably put a hex on us. You know how they are." She grabs Bubble Gum by the arm and drags her to their shitty hatchback.

Bubble Gum never takes her eyes off me. "If I don't hear nothin', I'm telling the sheriff all about you."

This chick and those damn double negatives. "Thought the whole town already knew?"

In the bedroom, Anora sits perched on the pillow like Her Highness has summoned me to perform.

Three strides across the bedroom, and she's in my arms. "I need some time away from you, Anora." As I toss her into the closet, I say, "You can't be trusted."

My hand grips the bathroom doorknob and time stands still. "I am nothing like her."

And digging a grave for a half-eaten raccoon goes a lot quicker than expected. My little raccoon friend is in and covered before my freshly washed hair is dry.

"I'm sorry she made me eat you, little buddy. You deserved better."

On the way back something gnaws at me. Is this my life? Eating raccoons. Running around naked, covered in blood and fur. Disposing of two bodies in less than a week. Sure, one was a raccoon, but still. What the fuck?

This tailspin needs to stop. The point of this is to write. When was the last time I put words on the page? Something needs to change. This calls for drastic measures.

With the phone pressed against my ear, the voice-mail on the other side greets me. The voice is familiar. Comforting. A bowl of tomato soup and a grilled cheese sandwich. "I know you've been calling me. Sorry. Pages were pouring out of me. I'm calling to see if you would be interested in coming out to visit. I know you have work, and you're probably mad at me. I deserve it. Call me back. Miss you."

My mom would say the best friends are the ones who pass through like ships in the night.

And finally, a chance to sit. My back is against the closet door. Anora remains locked in her prison of faded jeans and graphic tees.

"I'm going out. Figured I should show my face so this town knows I've got nothing to hide. You can sit in there and think about what you made me do."

Fighting with someone you love can be a messy business.

And the giant sign over the park reads:

Briar Springs Apple Festival

It's a small-town tradition full of pie contests and fundraising. A perfect place to show my face as if nothing has happened. Nothing says normal quite like high-calorie fried foods and laughing at dunk tank victims.

The kettle corn booth lures me over and within seconds the old man with the American Flag shirt and matching shorts hands me a warm bag of kettle corn. In return, he gets eight bucks.

A perfect mix of salt and sugar coats my tongue as handful after handful gets shoveled into my face hole.

Ten feet away, my green-haired lover chats with a lady dipping apples into caramel. Her back is to me.

Nerves wreck my composure. There is no shelter. No way to vanish.

Oh shit, she's turning around.

The only thing left to do is hide. There's only one black chick in this town, and she's fucked her. This apple cider booth is a perfect refuge.

Who knew there were so many variations of apple cider? Spiced cider sounds delicious.

"Why didn't you come say hi?"

The voice is behind me, but I know it belongs to her. It's a fair question. To be honest, my brain can't formulate an answer. I turn to her and say, "I don't know how these things work."

She looks amazing. The tank top and ripped jeans. The shell-toe Adidas. Her hair pulled back in a ponytail.

She says, "Friendships? They're pretty simple."

"I'm talking about the," I whisper, "client-type thing."

She feigns shock. "You don't consider us friends?" She leans into my ear and whispers, "You came all over me."

This woman knows how to worm her way into all my dirty thoughts. "I didn't want to overstep any boundaries. Break any codes of conduct."

She laughs until something catches her eye. "Jackpot!" She grabs my arm and drags me over to an apple pie booth.

It's so wholesome my head might explode.

The apple pie lady greets us with a smile. She's sixty and radiates a fake warmth perfected from decades of dinner parties and multi-level marketing schemes.

My green-haired lover says, "Two slices of apple pie. Oh, and could you warm them up, please?"

"My pleasure." With surgical precision, apple pie lady sticks two pieces of pie into her little toaster oven.

My green-haired lover turns and helps herself to my kettle corn. "This will be the best apple pie you've ever had."

Another handful of kettle corn finds its way into my face. "Bold statement."

My green-haired lover pulls out some cash. "Dinner's on me."

"Thanks!" As soon as there's room in my mouth for more words to get strung together, I say, "Wait, this is your dinner?"

"It's the only reason I come to this thing."

"And here I was hoping you came to see me."

She hands apple pie lady the cash. "If I had known you were going to be here, that would have been the reason."

Apple pie lady delivers the two pieces of warmed-up apple pie. My green-haired lover doesn't hesitate. Her plastic fork balances the hunk of pie until it gets delivered into her mouth. Between bites of warm pie, she mumbles, "One of these days you're gonna tell me what apples you use in this thing."

Apple pie lady waves off the absurd request. "Don't count on it."

It's difficult balancing the slice of pie and the kettle corn, but nothing gets dropped or wasted. My smile lets her know how harmless I am. "Thank you."

The excursion has morphed into a date, and it's okay with me. We walk amongst the children and families. We pass a booth with leatherwork. At another booth, we stop to admire the two dozen types of jerky.

Rabbit jerky. Shark jerky. Turtle jerky. Python jerky.

The pie has exceeded expectations and this sorry excuse for a fork can't get it in my mouth fast enough. "This is amazing."

Her lips, glossy from the buttery crust, my green-haired lover says, "Told you."

I gush, "There's over 2,500 varieties of apples grown in the United States. But only the crabapple is native to North America."

She seems shocked by my torrent of apple facts. It's unclear to both of us why those words spewed out of my mouth.

She asks, "You some kind of apple expert?"

"Nope. But I am an oracle of useless knowledge."

The last of her apple pie sits on her fork. Ready to meet its fate inside her mouth. "There's no such thing as useless knowledge." The fork disappears into her mouth and her apple pie is no more.

"Most people say it's weird."

There's a quick roll of her eyes as she chews the last of her pie. "Great spirits have always encountered violent opposition from mediocre minds."

There's still a few bites of pie left on my plate. For now, my tongue savors the buttery goodness of what's already in my mouth. "First Anne Sexton, now Einstein."

"Surprised to hear it from a stripper?"

"That's not what I meant."

She swings around so her body blocks my path. "It's on my refrigerator." Our eyes lock. The aroma of apple pie hangs between us. "I gotta get going. I'm on stage in like thirty."

My lips are desperate to taste the secondhand cinnamon that covers her mouth. The game is on. Which of us will make the first move in front of all these people? These disapproving eyes. Does the entire festival want to know which of us will break first? My skin is on alert. Touch me. Anywhere. Even a finger on my forearm will send a charge through me.

My green-haired lover leans in. We kiss. Cinnamon coats our lips. A gift we share.

We should grab each other's hands and race away. Vanish to somewhere private where we can finish this.

Away from all these prying eyes. A place where we can share more than cinnamon and pie residue.

Instead, our lips pull apart. Neither of us knows what to do next. That wasn't a kiss between a client and her service provider.

That was two people who want to argue about what type of pizza to order.

That was two people who spend rainy days reading books on the couch.

That was two people who want to go on road trips together and make fun of the souvenir mugs at the gas station.

Finally, my green-haired lover says, "Okay."

I reply, "Okay."

To which she replies, "Okay." She backpedals. Her eyes never leave mine. "Thanks for hanging out with me."

And with a flip of the switch, the bedroom plunges into darkness. Exhaustion washes over me. The blanket hugs my body and puts my mind at ease. The taste of apple pie lingers in my mouth. "Goodnight Anora."

Ideas hit me like a torrential downpour. They're not fully formed. They rarely are. Inspiration at its most raw and exciting. Some of these ideas are golden. Some aren't worth a damn. But sorting them will be the work of future Canna. Right now, it's important not to lose them. No time to sleep.

Moonlight trickles into the kitchen. Notecards and rolls of tape cover the kitchen table. Characters and ideas get scribbled. Phrases and fragments of dialogue get taped to the wall. Plot points and props. My hand can't write fast enough.

Has my green-haired lover become my green-haired muse? Was it the kiss? It certainly wasn't the apple pie. They say when you're not in a creative space, take a walk. Fresh air gets the creative juices flowing.

As does love.

This is crazy talk. This isn't love. We've only had sex once. Even that was a transaction. Money doesn't exchange hands in matters of the heart.

This is more carnal.

Another notecard is complete and taped to the wall with a dozen others.

Why question this? Isn't this the reason for the trip? To get some writing done.

A story comes together on the wall. Scribbled on the notecards are words like:

Porn costume shop
Electric blue
Strip club
Jasmine
A rusted pickup truck
Silent cries loud thoughts

This could be the ramblings of a crazy person. The Boyfriend will be here tomorrow. Hopefully, his visit won't hinder my progress.

It's only right I tell Anora he's coming to town. It's what friends do. We communicate. My back is against the closet door. Knees pulled tight to my chest. This is going to be a hard conversation to have, but she has to know. We need to re-establish trust. She needs to know she can't hurt him, no matter how jealous she is.

My tone hits the right note of forceful, yet caring. "I want you to know my boyfriend will be here sometime tomorrow. I may have called him to spite you. I hope you understand why I can't take you out until I know in my heart you won't try to hurt him. Or me."

My mom would say the fable about the scorpion and the frog is the closest she ever got to religion.

And the sound of a car horn grabs my heart and drags me to the front porch. The Boyfriend's spotless mid-sized BMW sits in the same spot the pickup truck occupied.

How long ago was it? Years?

The Boyfriend greets me with open arms. He wants me to give him a slow-motion run like the tearful couple at the end of a low-budget Christmas movie.

Instead, my strides are long and brisk. He engulfs me in his arms. The stench of Flaming Hot Cheetos assaults my nostrils. Our lips touch and his tongue infiltrates my mouth. The heat from the Cheetos is in my nose and mouth. It's not the only thing my taste receptors have identified. There's something subtle in there. A food he ate before the Flaming Hot Cheetos took over.

Is it Cool Ranch Doritos?

My tongue retreats, and we separate. The grimace on my face is involuntary, but he notices.

He smirks. "Sorry babe. Had some snacks on the way out."

Once inside, The Boyfriend takes it all in. His face is awash with concern and amusement. It's an odd mix. But when you see it from his perspective, the place does have a domestic terrorist vibe.

He's trying to figure out how many notecards there are. His lips move when he counts.

He asks, "Did you have to take out a loan to buy all these notecards?"

"It's part of my process. You hungry? I can make something."

Finally, his attention is back on me. "I was hoping to take you out and explore the town a bit."

"Aren't you tired from the drive? I'm more than happy to make something."

"I'm fine. Let's get out. Give you a chance to show me some of the local cuisine."

And The Boyfriend's favorite food is pizza. Sausage and black olives, to be exact. If it's thin crust and crispy, he might even do a dance. When we passed the place, he almost broke his neck trying to get a better view. He hardly gave me a chance to talk him into seafood.

So here we are. Dining at the former employer of the bartender who met his demise at my hands.

On the wall, above a picture of the bartender's face, a sign reads:

Prey for me

Two medium pizzas sit in front of us. One is a Margherita pizza. The other features sausage and black olives. They don't do thin crust.

The replacement bartender has been drying the same pint glass for seven minutes. In order for her to see it's dry, she'd have to stop staring a hole through my face.

All around us, the townies guzzle beer, eat pizza, and nibble on wings. It's remarkable how they're able to do this while never taking their eyes off us.

Is it because seeing a black person is like seeing a unicorn?

Is it because we're an interracial couple?

Is it because they believe the black chick killed the bartender?

Or is it all the above?

The Boyfriend tears off half a slice in one bite. Mid-chew, he uses his head to motion to the poster. "They spelled *"pray"* with an *"e"*."

"Give them a pass. Their friend is missing."

The Boyfriend takes a sip of his domestic beer and glances at the pint glass. "Is there a hair in here?"

There's a fifty percent chance it's intentional.

He takes another sip. As he sits the pint glass on the table, he says, "I didn't want to make this whole trip about me. I know you're writing, but I've got some good news."

He glances around the restaurant. Does he sense the eyeballs on us?

He says, "I got the promotion. The responsibility is a little daunting. As soon as I got word, my lizard brain kicked in and told me to flee."

A brief smile to let him know how proud I am. "When we drop fear, we can draw nearer to people, we can draw nearer to the earth, we can draw nearer to all the heavenly creatures surrounding us."

"That on one of your notecards?"

"It's from bell hooks." His face is a blank slate. I say, "She's an author."

"Right. Well, with the promotion comes a raise. A substantial raise. I'm looking to get a bigger place. Something big enough for two."

"Are you getting a dog?"

The look he gives me suggests a dog was not his plan.

The clanging of coins and dollars against tin ushers in a welcome distraction.

Next to us, the replacement bartender shakes a coffee tin full of spare change and dollars. She spits the words out with biting sarcasm. "We're accepting donations for our missing friend. He takes care of his sick aunt. Since he's been missing, we've been trying to help her with groceries and stuff. Care to donate?"

The Boyfriend produces a dollar. He tosses it into the tin.

The only cash in my purse is two twenties. The replacement bartender eyes me as my forty bucks makes it into the tin.

She says, "How generous of you."

As she makes her way to the next table, The Boyfriend says, "Forty bucks? You're making me look like a cheapskate."

"Nobody told you to only put in a dollar."

"I'm visiting."

My mom would say sports give us a reason to hate each other.

And The Boyfriend lies next to me. His heels touch my heels. My eyes are on the closet. He rolls over and spoons me. An arm comes over and cups my breast. His lips leave a damp spot on my shoulder.

Last time Anora was in the closet when things got hot and heavy, my raccoon friend became breakfast. "Not tonight, babe."

He sighs like a toddler and takes half the sheets with him when he rolls back over.

Time melts away and his snores tell me he's asleep. My eyes are wide open and glued to the closet. Is our squabble over? Can we trust each other?

A loud knock pulls me into an upright position. A glance at The Boyfriend confirms my suspicions. He's still asleep.

Another knock.

My eyes scan the darkness until they land on the closet door.

Another knock.

It's not the closet. It's not even in the bedroom.

The Boyfriend remains fast asleep.

Out of the bed and across the bedroom. My hand opens the door. There's a creek as the outdated hinges bemoan the disturbance. A step into the blackness of the hallway.

This entire place is only fifteen hundred square feet. The main room is only a dozen steps away. The moon has the night off. What remains is the blackness of night.

In the kitchen, the light shudders to life. Nothing out of the ordinary here.

A check of the cabinets delivers nothing.

The drawers seem normal.

Nothing strange in the fridge.

The knocks have ceased. Only the dark void of nothingness fills the air.

The kitchen lights provide illumination in the living room. It's not much, but it'll do. Eyes closed and my body waits for another knock that never comes.

"Canna?"

In the door frame stands The Boyfriend. Half asleep. More confused than worried. He says, "What are you doing?"

"I heard something."

He yawns. "And you didn't wake me?"

"It's probably a raccoon or whatever."

He shuffles towards the front door. "Let me do some recon. Confirm your suspicions."

It's late, and he can't even see straight. I grab his hand and say, "It's fine. Let's go back to bed."

And The Boyfriend hunts for any program involving a ball and scoring points. He yells into the kitchen, "I'm excited about what you have going on right now."

Flour covers my forehead, arms and hands. The fury of my whisking sends a plume of flour mist into the air. "I know how you love foods that absorb syrup."

By the sounds of it, Operation Sports Ball is over. Instead, he's settled on the local news. Some police officer in the middle of a press conference says, "The young man has been missing from the neighboring town of Briar Springs."

Great.

The Boyfriend pays no attention. "Having a dog could be fun."

The police officer says, "We are in contact with the local officials in that town."

"But we should get a dog big enough to scare off any unwanted intruders. How about a pit bull?"

The police officer says, "We have made this a priority."

Could they be coming here? There's nothing to point them in my direction. Is there?

The Boyfriend continues. "I know they have a bad rep, but there are no bad dogs. Only bad owners."

There's no evidence here. The place is clean. It's been a while. Even if there were fingerprints, they're long gone by now.

Oh crap.

The Boyfriend hears me open the back door. He asks, "Where ya headed?"

The grill remains open from the night of the incident. What's left of the steaks remains on the grate. Maggots fight over the charred remnants.

Time to get rid of the evidence.

Maggots cling to my hands and the steaks as the lake comes into view. The weaker maggots plummet to the ground. The moment the lake is in range, the steaks get tossed into the water.

And The Boyfriend performs the first part of his sleep routine.

At the edge of the bed, I don't even turn from the closet as I say, "I hate to ask you this, but do you mind sleeping on the couch? After last night with the noises, It would put me at ease."

"Not a problem." He gurgles and spits.

"Thank you."

The Boyfriend is out of the room. Presumably on the couch, keeping watch for some malevolent entity.

We have the bedroom to ourselves. It's good to have her in my arms. We face each other and I whisper, "I never should have put you in there. You spend your whole life telling yourself you'll never be like your mother and one day you wake up and that's exactly who you are."

It's been a while since sleep came this easy. The slumber lasts for two hours. The Boyfriend's presence is in the air. Lurking. Anora confirms he's in here with us. He won't say anything now. He'll mention it when he needs to go nuclear. Patience is the reason he got the promotion. For now, my eyes stay closed.

We'll deal with it later.

My mom would say there
are no happy endings
without someone's demise.

And my note to The Boyfriend is brief yet to the point.
Three words. Be. Back. Later. He'll see it when he
gets out of the shower.

Her excitement was palpable. It was all over her voice.
We played it cool, but my heart was pounding. Hers was
too. Even through the phone, it was obvious. Short sentences and one-word answers before the question was
complete.

My car proceeds along the gravel road of the trailer
park. The HOA must have a bylaw requiring residents
to populate their yards with plastic animals and chubby
gnomes. The car gets parked next to the Jeep. Halfway to
the door, she greets me with a kiss.

The inside of the trailer is immaculate. Even the items on the floor seem to belong there. Books line the shelves. The artwork is steampunk erotica. If there is such a thing.

My green-haired lover closes the door and is all over me within seconds. Her hands grope my ass. Her tongue dances with mine. She pulls me in so close our nipples rub through our shirts.

She comes up for air long enough to ask, "What's in the bag?"

I open my backpack and say, "I didn't have time to buy any toys, so I was hoping you could play dress up again. I brought money."

She takes the outfit from me. "Keep your money."

First, her tank top comes off. There's nothing underneath it. She shimmies out of her pants. There's nothing under those either. She stands before me, naked. It's hard to tell which of us enjoys this more. My green-haired lover welcomes my gaze, and these eyes of mine are happy to oblige.

Equal parts anticipation and dread surge through me. Anticipation, because this moment has played in my head on an infinite loop for days on end. Dread, because my true desire could be a step too far.

Promises were made, and they must be upheld.

My green-haired lover adjusts the blue wig and poses. I tell her I love it.

She leads me to the couch and pulls me on top of her. Her hands work their way under my yoga pants and lower them until the air cools my ass. I move her hands and say, "Wait."

My green-haired lover watches me dig through my backpack. She purrs, "What do you have?"

Found her. I pull Anora out of the backpack and present her to my green-haired lover. "I want to introduce you to somebody."

My green-haired lover bolts upright.

"This is my friend, Anora."

"Your friend?"

This isn't going well. We take a step towards her for reassurance. "It's okay. I talked to her on the way over."

"What is happening right now?"

We're on the couch. To comfort her, my hand finds its way onto her leg. "I told her watching us would help with her jealousy."

My green-haired friend brushes my hand off her leg and jumps to her feet. "Why are you talking about the doll like it's a person?"

"Her name is Anora. I told you. She's my friend." My outstretched hand gets slapped away.

"Friend? Is this some sort of joke?"

"This is about us. All of us."

"You turned me into a sex surrogate for your doll?"

Nothing could be further from the truth. My arms tighten around Anora to let her know it's okay.

The stripper says, "You have some serious issues."

"What? No. No. No. You're confused. I told her all about us. I explained to her how if she gets to know you, she'll see how special you are to me."

Tears well in the corners of the stripper's eyes. "I'm not gonna be part of your sick little game, Canna."

It's all going to shit. Anora was right. She's never going to understand. "Game? What are you —"

"Get out!" The stripper takes off the wig and throws it at me. The shirt and pants come off. Both get thrown at me. Naked, the stripper marches to the door and opens it. "Take your creepy ass doll and get out."

With the outfit and wig in my hand, we make our way to the door. "Her name is Anora."

My mom would say my best thoughts are the ones she gave me.

And there's hardly anybody at the diner. Not sure why we're back by the bathrooms, but it's where they stuck us. Anora is in a high chair across from me. I lower the menu and say, "Thanks for not hurting the stripper. I know you could have."

Part of me wants breakfast, but we're on the cusp of the afternoon. I should eat something to signify the progress of the day. I say, "You were right about her. I should have listened to you."

Hair Bun is working today. It's unclear if we're in her section because nobody has come over to help us. When she gets close enough, I say, "We asked for two menus but the hostess only gave us one."

She doesn't budge. Instead, she shifts her judgmental eyes between me and Anora.

It's obvious what's on her mind. I say, "One for each of us." With an extra side of sarcasm, I add, "Thank you."

She saunters off.

There's three or four things on the menu that would ease the pain and guilt from this morning. "I want something fried."

There's a scream from the kitchen. Right behind the counter. It's Hair Bun. Both of her hands are in the fryer. The hot grease pours over the side of the baskets.

Her screams persist. Why can't she take her hands out? Did she do this to herself? It's hard to tell exactly how or why she submerged both hands into the fryer.

One glance at Anora and my questions get answered.

The sound of searing flesh has the attention of the entire diner. Singed hair from her arms takes over as the predominant smell. A tattooed cook grabs Hair Bun and yanks her away from the fryer. Grease and melting flesh drip down her arms. The blisters and bubbles form in real time, each pops as they reach maximum expansion.

People race over to check on Hair Bun. The commotion provides a perfect diversion for us to make our escape.

And at the town's grocery store, we arrive at Bubble Gum's register. I place the economy-sized bleach on the conveyor belt and say, "I've got a stain I need to get rid of."

Bubble Gum smacks her gum. "I know it was you." She eyes the bleach before twisting off the cap and removing the protective seal. The container makes it to her mouth.

A woman in line behind me says, "Christ! What are you doing?"

Bubble Gum doesn't even flinch. She puts the bleach to her lips and chugs it. Gulp after gulp, bleach spills out the sides of her mouth.

We head to the door. She continues to chug the bleach as we pass her. "Somebody help this woman. She's drinking bleach, for God's sake."

Hopefully, that was convincing enough.

My mom would say the voices in her head are the only ones she trusts.

And The Boyfriend greets us from the sofa the moment we step in.

He says, "You and the doll catch a matinee?"

"I was getting inspired."

The Boyfriend leans back. "Enough with the riddles."

"That was a statement. Your confusion doesn't make it a riddle."

"Did you ask me to sleep on the couch so you could sleep with the doll?"

Not all comments deserve a response. The Boyfriend follows me into the kitchen. His voice is full of concern. "I'm worried about you."

My laptop is on the kitchen table. He needs to know he's not my priority at the moment. Anora sits across from me as the laptop buzzes to life.

He's relentless. "You never mentioned dolls or collected dolls. Out of nowhere, you're sleeping with a doll? You carrying it into town with you?"

"I don't need your help, Anora."

The Boyfriend glares at me. He seems confused. "Canna. Is Anora the doll?"

My focus remains on the work. Eventually, he'll get the hint and leave us alone.

He leans on the table. His muscles tense. "Why are you acting like this?" he says.

"I'm saving your life."

"Forget it. I'm outta here."

The beginning of my book has a few hiccups, but the first act shows promise. If The Boyfriend wants to leave, it's his decision.

He opens the front door, and there's a moment of silence before he asks if there's something he can help them with.

Who the hell is on the other side of the door? What could they need help with?

The book will have to wait. Anora stays in the kitchen. In the living room are the sheriff and his deputy. The Boyfriend closes the door and joins them.

All six of their eyes are on me.

The sheriff glares at me. "Ma'am."

"Hello."

The deputy takes in the walls full of notecards. The place checks all the boxes for the lair of a serial killer.

The sheriff scowls at The Boyfriend. "Who are you?"

"I'm her boyfriend."

The sheriff is not happy about this new revelation. He bites the insides of his cheek and refuses to make eye contact as he speaks to me. Instead, his focus is on the wall. "Like to ask you a few questions about Bryson Elliott." He shows us a picture of the bartender's grinning rapist face.

The Boyfriend connects the dots. "The pizza guy?"

The sheriff is more than happy to turn his attention to The Boyfriend. "So, you know him?"

The Boyfriend says, "No. We saw his picture when we were having dinner. They were taking a collection."

Finally, the sheriff gives me his attention. "It's my understanding you know him. That true?"

"More or less."

The sheriff straightens his back. "I'm gonna need you to explain the nature of your relationship."

The deputy steps towards a wall for a closer look at a notecard. I shift my attention off the sheriff and place it on the deputy. "I met him at the bar. I wanted a pizza. He took my order. Nothing scandalous."

"But you invited him over. Did you not?"

The Boyfriend latches on and turns to me. "You invited him over?"

The sheriff gets a kick out of this bit of bonus drama. He says, "Did you have sexual intercourse with Bryson Elliott?"

The satisfaction in his voice makes my stomach turn. "No. I did not."

The Sheriff smirks. "Are you sure?"

"If there's a doctor around, they're welcome to swab my vagina."

The sheriff takes out a pen and his notepad. He flips the notepad open with a bit too much flair. He's enjoying this way too much. "Did you buy condoms the day he went missing?"

The Boyfriend's face turns red. His fists clench. "You wanted to fuck him?"

"I don't know when he went missing."

The sheriff says, "The last time he was heard from, he was making plans to come see you."

There's no saving the relationship with The Boyfriend. Calling him here was a terrible idea. The only thing left is to stay out of prison. "Did you also know I returned the condoms because he never came over?"

The sheriff says, "Sounds like you intended to have sex with him?"

It's difficult to tell if the goal is to solve the case or destroy my relationship with The Boyfriend.

The deputy takes a step towards The Boyfriend. "Sheriff, I'm gonna take him out for further questioning. Let you focus on her."

"Go ahead."

The deputy and The Boyfriend step outside. The moment the door closes, I say, "Can we take this into the kitchen so we can talk in private?"

"They're outside. How much more privacy do you need?"

There's no point in arguing with this man. I head into the kitchen and say, "Is this about a missing person, or do you like hearing about my sex life?"

He follows me into the kitchen. His hand hovers over his holster. "Right now, your sex life is a key factor in finding out what happened to this young man."

He eyeballs Anora and keeps his hand over his gun. "I see you still got your doll."

"We're friends."

"You and the doll?"

Something in his voice urges me to grab a knife out of the butcher block.

"Lower the knife, or I will shoot you."

I turn to face him and say, "You shouldn't have said that, sheriff."

His teeth grind and his body shakes. His hand clutches the gun at his side.

He yells out. "Junior!"

This is Anora's doing.

He has the gun. We have his thoughts.

"How are you doing this to me?"

I test the edge of the knife with my thumb. "Doing what?"

The sweat beads on his forehead. The Boyfriend and the deputy race into the kitchen.

The deputy goes for his gun. "What's going on?"

The sheriff turns, lifts his gun, and fires a round into the deputy's head. Blood and brain matter cover the walls, the floor, and The Boyfriend. The deputy's body drops. Blood seeps out of the wound and spreads across the floor.

The Boyfriend wipes a chunk of brain off his face. "Sheriff?"

The sheriff points his gun at The Boyfriend.

I yell, "Anora no!"

The gun shakes in the sheriff's hand. A brief glance at Anora and now the gun is at his own temple. He pulls the trigger. Blood covers the wall and his lifeless body hits the floor.

The Boyfriend races towards me. "What the fuck just happened?"

"It's best you leave."

Two steps away from me, and he stops. "Is this your doing?"

At war with my mind. Which thoughts are mine and which are hers? My hand raises the knife.

The Boyfriend says, "Canna, put the knife down."

These eyes are still mine, and they're pooling with tears. "Please. You need to leave."

"You don't want to hurt me."

"I don't." With the knife, I point to Anora and say, "She does." He needs to go if he wants to live. She's winning. Less and less of these thoughts belong to me.

He eyes the doll. Don't do it, you idiot. Put the macho bullshit aside and save yourself.

He doesn't leave.

Instead, he charges me. We're locked in an embrace. He hugs me tight for a moment. When he leans back, his eyes are as big as saucers.

All I can say is, "I'm so sorry."

She didn't want to make me do it. Instead, she made him do it to himself. When he takes a step back, the knife slides out of his rib cage.

The red spot on his shirt grows bigger and bigger. His hand goes to the wound, but the stain grows around it.

The Boyfriend falls to a knee. "Did the doll make you want to fuck him?"

My attention is on Anora. "Don't you dare try to stop me."

His keys are on the corner of the kitchen counter. I help The Boyfriend to his feet. "I swear I'll come right back to you, Anora. Trust me."

The Boyfriend's blood covers me as we hobble across the yard and to his car. I get the door open and tell him to get to a hospital.

His voice is weak. "If the doll is doing this, come with me. I forgive you... for everything."

"Her name is Anora."

My mom would say lying to yourself is the truest form of blasphemy.

And the blood on the floor warms my bare feet. The stench from the bodies fills the air. There's no time to worry about them. It's only a matter of time before more cops arrive and this chick has a book to write.

The laptop comes to life, and it's time to get busy. An hour later and the next ten pages are complete.

Anora sits across from me. We're in this together.

After three hours, the book is forty pages long. The next section needs some consideration. It's what the note-cards are for.

A cup of tea will get this train on the move again.

Many of the notecards are hard to read because of the blood and brains smeared all over them. There are a few instances where the blood needs to be wiped off. Despite the streak of red, the cards are legible enough.

A bloody notecard sits next to the laptop and my fingers get back to work. A half hour later and ten more pages are done.

The knock at the door wrecks my flow. Would the cops knock? What if it's not the cops?

The smart choice would be to avoid it. But my curiosity wins out.

My hand turns the doorknob, and the door opens enough for me to peek out.

It's not the cops.

It's the stripper. Eyes puffy from crying.

She can't see the carnage. My body slides out, and the door shuts behind me.

The stripper asks, "Why is there a cop car in your front yard?"

"I don't know. Some training thing in the woods. They asked if they could park here." The lies flow out of me. Are these Anora's words? Are they mine?

There's no telling anymore.

The stripper says, "Are you lying to me?"

"Now I'm a liar?"

She glances at the cars in the front yard, turns back to me. "I don't like the way we left things. If you want somebody to talk to, I'm here for you."

"I'll call you, or whatever." My words cause her to flinch. She tries to be strong, but her eyes betray her.

She tries to take my hand. "Are you in trouble?"

My hand rests on hers. It's good to touch her. I rub her fingers with mine. "Wait here."

My mind races. At first, the search fails. The bedroom is a mess. Clothes cover the floor and bed. But there it is. Under a shirt on the dresser. It's in my hand and my heart beats faster than ever before.

She's still on the front porch. Thank god. She forces a smile. "Thought you left me."

My hand flips hers over so her palm faces the sky. I place the scorpion brooch in her hand and close it. "Please, keep this."

"What is it? She gives it a closer examination.

I tell her it's a gift. Passed from woman to woman and now it's hers. I tell her I want her to remember me. I tell her she's going to hear things, but she should ignore them.

"You're scaring me."

I tell her she needs to go. Now.

"Come with me."

I tell her I can't. I have to finish my book.

She doesn't budge. She doesn't know this is me saving her life. How do you explain you're saving someone from something you may or may not do at any moment?

Her hand comes for me, but my body recoils. Her glazed eyes meet mine. "Why are you acting like this?"

"I don't know if this is love or lust. But either way, you deserve better than me."

My green-haired friend eyes the brooch and says, "Whatever it is, we can face it together. It can't be that bad."

She needs to go. If Anora gets jealous, anything could happen. "Thing is, if you don't leave, she may force me to kill you. I'm trying to avoid that. Now go."

My green-haired friend takes the hint and backpedals to her Jeep. Her eyes never leave mine. She opens the Jeep without even a glance at the door. Stripes of mascara cover her face. "I hope you rot in hell, bitch."

As long as it's after this book is done.

And Anora sits patiently. She's agreed to leave me alone and let me work.

"This is the story I've been waiting for."

Three hundred pages done.

If you have issues in your story, the third act is when they rear their scornful little heads.

Around two-thirty in the morning the fatigue sets in. Producing this many pages in this short of time is taxing. How long has this been going on? Twelve hours? Five days?

The rumbling in my stomach tells me food wouldn't be a bad idea.

Three hundred and ten pages complete.

The manuscript comes first. But breakfast food would be amazing. Are there ingredients here for pancakes?

Three hundred and twenty pages complete.

My eyes are barely open. The throbbing behind my ears intensifies.

"How long have I been at it, Anora?"

Three hundred and twenty-five pages complete.

Fingers cramp. The prose gets loose. Mistakes creep into the sentences. Silly mistakes. Using the wrong form of "their." Forgetting punctuation.

"I don't know how much longer this can go on."

Three hundred and twenty-nine pages complete.

Water will help with the cramping.

Three hundred and thirty pages complete.

The water is cold and delicious. It's exactly what my body needed. Getting away from the table and the laptop reinvigorates me.

Back to work. The story is nearly complete. The march to the climax has me excited.

The stench from the dead bodies is unbearable. It's been so long they've started to rot.

Three hundred and forty pages complete.

Blue and red lights flood the cabin.

Three hundred and forty-two pages complete.

This can only mean one thing.

Three hundred and forty-three pages complete.

We're so close. We have to finish.

Three hundred and forty-four pages complete.

"This is the Clay County police department. Come out with your hands up."

And the reflection in the mirror is the black chick version of Anora. The red tracksuit pants are snug, but they'll do. The white T-shirt could use a wash. The wig is loose, but the pins keep it in place.

The smell of jasmine hangs in the air. What I did to her makes my soul ache. My green-haired friend is better off without me. She'll understand soon enough.

Anora is in my arms and we stare at our reflection in the mirror.

We make it into the kitchen. The blood on the walls, the bodies on the floor. The stench in the air.

They're going to have a field day with this.

There's no time for me to reflect on what happened. No time for celebration. My hands slam the laptop shut. They'll want it for evidence.

Hand in hand, we make our way to the front door. The cool air hits me as we step outside. The darkness is serene.

I'm floored by the number of guns pointed at us. Law enforcement officers hide behind open car doors with their weapons drawn.

Anora is against my chest. We face them together, ready for whatever is about to happen.

The officers shake. Some even cry. They fight against themselves. Their guns quiver. Some officers squeeze their eyes shut.

"Anora, don't."

All of the officers point their weapons at each other.

This will be a massacre.

"They've done nothing to deserve this, Anora."

With Anora in my arms, we take a step closer. The officers keep their guns trained on each other. A few of the officers weep.

"I'm here to turn myself in. Nobody has to get hurt. And nobody has to die."

This dashcam footage is going viral.

Anora has them. It's obvious. They won't even look my way. Their focus is on each other. We arrive at the closest squad car. I put her on the hood of the car and say, "Anora, let them do their jobs."

Anora pulls a power move, and the officers cock their weapons.

"This can't continue, Anora. It has to end here."

The officer's guns point skyward.

"Anora!"

One by one, the officers point their guns at their own temples.

"If you care about me, you'll let them arrest me."

If this doesn't get through to her, nothing will. There's going to be bodies all over the front yard. We'll have to go on the run. Nobody will believe the dash cam and body cam footage. They'll never stop hunting us, no matter how many bodies we leave in our wake.

This has to stop now.

"Anora!"

One officer lowers his gun.

Then another.

And another.

Before long, they lower their guns. They waste no time. Blood-shot eyes and tear-streaked faces tackle me to the ground. Knees dig into my back. They pull my arms backwards. There's a boot on my face. Dirt fills my mouth, eyes, and nostrils. The handcuffs are cold against my wrists.

Anora gets dropped into an evidence bag while they shove me into the back of a squad car.

My mom would say the great ones are always persecuted.

After

And this place smells as wretched as it looks. A foul mix of mildew, urine, and feces. The lights alone are enough to drive you insane. At night, the halls fill with screams and the poetry of my fellow lunatics.

The stories suggest residents who never made it out roam the asylum. Spirits trapped in the last place they called home.

In a place like this, you don't want to make any friends. Some of these people are geniuses and their only goal is to worm their way into your head. The ones who aren't geniuses are insane. Humans who have slipped through the cracks.

They keep me at the end of the hall. My circumstances aren't as bad as some others. At least they let me move around in my cell. Across from me, they shackled the red-haired woman to the wall.

The air fills with dirty talk. When the guards come by, the women yell obscenities and offer themselves. Anything the guards want. Five minutes is all they need. Life in a cell can be lonely. Who knows how long it's been since any of these women have had a proper orgasm?

For me, it's been seven months. Give or take a few weeks.

The guard makes his way through the hall. Even with the catcalls and the occasional flash of dirty breasts, his eyes remain forward. The person beside him comes into view. This should be interesting. My first visitor.

When he and the guard arrive at my cell, I say, "Thanks for coming. I don't get a lot of visitors."

The agent says, "Figured it was time to show you this." He presses the book against the glass. The cover is minimalist and creepy. Not my favorite cover, but it represents the book well.

The cover reads:

Anora
By
Canna Wendle

I ask him what happened to the original title, "A Certain Calmness"?

He says, "Too artsy." and adds, "Can I leave it here with you?"

A glance over at the guard. He remains stone-faced. I turn back to the agent and say, "You'll have to check at the front on your way out. They're pretty strict here."

"I've noticed."

One of my neighbors asks the agent to take off his pants. It's fun seeing him so uncomfortable.

Every man should have to endure this at least once in their life.

I ask, "How's my ex?"

"Good. Well, you know." The hurt on my face makes him break eye contact. "The publisher is ecstatic. They're saying you might have a shot at the bestseller list."

"Cool."

"Gotta say, never had you framed as a horror writer."

"It's the story that poured out of me."

He leans into the glass. As if what he's about to say is the real reason he ventured into this godforsaken place. He glances at the guard and back at me. "Got a phone call yesterday. A few movie studios want the rights to the book. Could be a nice payday."

"Who's gonna play me?"

"It's a little early for that." He sighs and takes a step back. His eyes seem... sad. "It was good seeing you, Canna."

"You too."

He turns and lets the guard lead him back down the hall.

I yell out, "Sorry about your cabin."

He turns back with a smile. "We all gotta sacrifice to make great art. Besides, thanks to you, I'm shopping for a place in the Hamptons."

We both laugh.

Never trust someone who gets paid by percentage.

The End

THE BIG DECAY

Prologue

Various shades of brown stain the walls of the seedy apartment building. The parts of the molding spared by the dust are chipped and smudged with god knows what.

Iris wills herself up the stairs. A thirty-five-year-old who doesn't look a day over fifty, her tank top is dirty and stained with sweat. The rips in her jeans aren't a design choice. Her blonde hair flops in various directions. She's a hot mess. She's also out of breath when she makes it to the fourth floor.

The carpet on the fourth floor has more stains than the walls. Iris saunters along until she arrives at apartment 407 and immediately bangs on the door.

No answer.

Frustrated, she bangs on the door once again. This time with more fervor.

From the other side of the door, Mitchell says, "Who is it?"

"Breezer sent me."

Mitchell opens the door, but the chain lock keeps it from opening too wide. One of Mitchell's blue eyes peers through the crack. The eye inspects Iris before the door slams shut.

A series of unlocking sounds from the inside until Mitchell opens the door fully. Iris sizes him up. A decent-looking guy if he would bathe on a regular basis. He motions for her to step inside.

Iris busts in like she owns the place.

Mitchell slams the door behind her. Iris takes in the apartment. The place is dingy. If the rats don't already live here, they're making plans to move in.

Iris finally turns to Mitchell. "Breezer sent me."

"You said that." He takes a step towards her and continues his inspection. "How is my old buddy Breezer? Haven't seen him in a while."

Iris digs in her pockets. "What do you say we get down to business? Breezer tells me you've got the goods. The pure stuff." She pulls out a wad of cash. "I've had a tough week mister and I'm looking to get straight. You wanna help me out or what?"

"Lose the shirt."

"What?"

Mitchell says, "The shirt. Take it off."

Iris rolls her eyes, takes off her shirt to expose her sweat-stained bra.

"Now the bra."

Iris undoes her bra. "Enjoying yourself?" She drops the bra to the floor and smirks.

Mitchell scans her body. "Turn."

She turns. After a full rotation, her gaze meets his.

Mitchell says, "I haven't seen Breezer in six weeks. Dropping his name raises alarm bells. I had to make sure you weren't wired for sound." He walks to the kitchen. "You can put your clothes back on."

Iris gathers her clothes.

Mitchell yells from the kitchen, "How much you got?"

Iris puts her bra on. "Seventy-five."

Mitchell returns from the kitchen with a baggie of heroin in his hand.

Iris slips her shirt on. She pulls the cash out of her pocket and hands it to Mitchell.

He takes the cash. After a cursory glance, he hands her the heroin.

Iris places the bag under her nose and inhales. Pure ecstasy as she exhales. "Can I push off here?"

"No."

#

The abandoned tire manufacturing plant is home to various unsavory activities. Moonlight pours in through broken windows and reflects off shards of glass. Dirty mattresses litter the floor. In the corner sits a pile of decapitated dolls.

Across from the doll altar, Iris fixes herself a hit. She boils the heroin on a bent spoon. Seconds later, a needle sucks it in. She flicks the needle with her finger and slaps her wrist until a vein responds. She licks her finger and uses the wetness to clear the grime off her skin. The needle penetrates the vein. Her head rolls back. Eyes do the same.

A smile as euphoria washes over her.

And then she coughs.

She coughs again.

A third, more forceful cough erupts out of her.

She's enveloped into a full-blown coughing fit. Her hands clutch her stomach. Her legs seize and she writhes in pain. Foamy blood bubbles out of her mouth.

One

Ouroboros occupies a spot in the heart of the city, but it's not visible from the streets. It sits under an upscale bar serving over-priced martinis. The entrance is sandwiched between two dumpsters. Once inside the door, the stairs descend into darkness.

Oroboros features gaudy, plush, Chinese decor. Pillows and throw cushions cover the floor. The entire place is arranged around the main attractions. Hookahs and opium pipes. There are no chairs. No tables. No couches.

Half the addicts smoke and lounge on the pillows and cushions. The other half are passed out.

Prostitutes of all ages and ethnicities carry trays and hookahs. A red-haired woman with pale skin, dressed in sheer lingerie, leads a man in a business suit into a back room.

Various pieces of original art populate the walls. Each piece features a snake eating its own tail. Passed out under one of these paintings is Blake Fields. A clean-shaven man in his forties. His red and black tie hangs loose around his neck. The sleeves on his white dress shirt are rolled to his elbows. The cracked and ashy corners of his hands suggest his brown skin could use a coat of cocoa butter.

He stirs and his eyelids pull apart. With a groan, he pulls himself into a sitting position and rubs the back of his hand across his face. His eyes search the surroundings until they land on his sports coat and jacket. He collects his things and stumbles out.

The morning light blinds Blake as he squeezes between the dumpsters and into the alley.

The city teems with sewer smoke and morning dew. Shop owners raise the graffiti-filled roll-up doors to expose their storefronts.

A woman comes into view. She's half a block ahead of Blake and she's headed straight for him. The woman growls. It's Iris. But now she's covered in blood and spider veins. Her eyes are bloodshot.

Another growl as she draws closer to Blake.

He glances over his shoulder. Contemplates making a run for it. Iris takes another step towards him. She's only a few feet away. He clocks her movements.

Her right ear falls off.

Blake sighs and takes a step back.

She growls and charges him.

In one motion, Blake whips out a butterfly knife, and opens it. Iris lunges for him. He braces her with a forearm against her throat.

She tries to bite him but the forearm keeps her mouth at a safe distance. With his other hand, he buries the butterfly knife into the top of her skull. She goes limp. Blake pulls the knife out. She falls to the ground. Dead.

He pulls himself to his knees. On the ground next to him is a damp club flyer promoting a DJ Rona Dice set this Friday night. He uses it to clean the knife.

#

This neighborhood coffee shop features mismatched furnishings. All the retro couches and chairs are occupied by hipsters on their laptops.

Blake places a newspaper on the counter. The headline reads:

HOMELESS MAN EATS FAMILY OF FOUR

The pierced barista makes her way over. Her eyes graze over the headline and make their way to Blake as he says, "They probably had it coming." The barista laughs as Blake continues. "Just the paper and a large green tea. Hot."

#

Blake strolls along the hallway of a dull office building with beige carpet and gray walls. Tea in one hand.

Newspaper in the other. He takes a sip of his green tea and stops.

At the end of the hall, a woman stands in front of a door. She checks her watch. Her blonde hair contrasts with her light brown skin. Her curves fill out the blue mini dress with the overt cleavage. She's dressed for attention. Whoever put the ring on her finger earns decent money.

When her eyes meet Blakes, she lowers them to the carpet. Her lack of confidence is odd considering how she's dressed. "Is this your office?"

Blake arrives next to her. "It is." His keys find their way into the door and they enter his office.

The place is a disaster. Fast food bags, manila folders, and random office supplies populate every available surface. A doorway leads to a makeshift bedroom with an adjoining bathroom. There's a small futon and a portable closet.

Scattered on the desk are dozens of black and white photos of a man and two women performing lewd sex acts. The photos were taken with a long-angle lens through a window. Most likely from across the street.

Before the woman in blue can make it to the pictures, Blake springs into action. He collects the black and whites and crams them into a desk drawer. "Excuse the mess. Workin' on a case."

"You are Blake Fields, correct?"

"I am." He tidies his desk. "What can I help you with?"

The woman in blue surveys the office. She's not impressed. "My name is Elizabeth Preston and I want you to trail my husband, Arthur Preston. I believe he's –"

She takes a moment to gather herself. "I suspect he's cheating on me and I want to know for sure." She fights back the tears preparing to march from her eyes to her cheeks. "If there's another woman involved, I want to know who she is and what they do. I have money. Name your price, Mr. Fields."

"Blake."

Elizabeth stiffens. "I prefer Mr. Fields."

"As long as I'm on your mind and in your mouth."

Elizabeth doesn't hide her disgust. "I am a married woman. This is not appropriate."

Blake leans back in his chair. "I'm talking about my name. What are you talking about?"

"You know what I'm talking about, Mr. Fields."

Blake feigns repulsion. "Mrs. Preston, this is a place of business. I would appreciate it if you treated it as such."

Elizabeth fails to hide her amusement. She covers by digging into her purse. "Do I pay now?"

Blake leans forward. "Half now. The rest when the job is done. The particulars will be in the contract." He pulls a contract and a pen out of the drawer. "I'll need some information from you. When it's done, I'll give you a call. Show you the results."

Two

A ten-year-old dented silver Toyota Camry sits in the middle of a suburban neighborhood. Blake sits behind the wheel. He stuffs a bacon, egg, and cheese breakfast burrito into his mouth. A Nikon Camera sits on the seat next to him.

Five houses down, a rotund, bookish black man in his fifties exits a home with blue shutters. He makes his way to the brand-new maroon sedan in the driveway. This is Arthur Preston.

Blake snaps pictures of the man as he gets into his car. Arthur starts the car and pulls out of the driveway.

Another bite of the burrito and Blake keys the ignition, puts the car in drive, and follows Arthur Preston.

#

Arthur maneuvers his car through the industrial part of town. He passes a derelict building with a mural of zombies attacking a school bus. Scrawled in graffiti above the mural it reads:

And The Children Laughed

Arthur pulls into a parking space and gets out of the car.

A block away, Blake pulls his car onto the side of the street. He snaps six pictures of Arthur as he heads into the building. Once Arthur vanishes, Blake takes a bite of his burrito.

#

The Scarlet Room is a burlesque club where the design choices reinforce its name. The walls are scarlet. The floor is scarlet. The ceiling is scarlet. Each couch, table, and chair is scarlet.

Well-dressed clientele mingle amongst cocktail waitresses. A trio of burlesque dancers perform on stage. Their black and white corsets stand out in a sea of scarlet.

Arthur Preston takes in the performance at the end of the bar. His eyes never leave the dancers as he sips his club soda.

On the opposite end of the bar sits Blake. The pink-haired bartender with the flowing locks, and a scarlet corset makes her way over as she dries a rocks glass. "What'll it be?"

Blake keeps his eyes on Arthur. "Whiskey. Old fashioned."

The bartender leaves to make the drink.

The performance concludes and the dancers shuffle off stage. Arthur can't hide his excitement. Something big is about to happen and he can't wait. The DJ changes the music to a sexy jazz-pop number.

Onto the stage struts Cinnamon. A twenty-five-year-old woman with a red-haired pixie cut, dark brown skin, and a slinky confidence. She's dressed in high heels, a thong, and pasties. Each movement is sultry. Every glance is seductive. She has the undivided attention of the entire club. Especially Arthur Preston.

Blake studies Arthur. But when he follows his gaze to Cinnamon, he has a hard time taking his eyes off her.

Cinnamon's dance concludes and the applause is deafening. She heads off stage in the same seductive manner she arrived with. Arthur gives her a standing ovation.

In the corner is a table full of scantily clad women. Amongst them sits Pettford. A man in his mid-forties who's dressed like the pimp in a Broadway musical. He whispers something into the ear of one of the women. She rushes backstage.

Arthur returns to his seat and takes a sip of his club soda. He grins as Cinnamon comes from backstage. She's changed into a corset and makes her way to Pettford. The other ladies give her room.

Cinnamon leans in and whispers something into Pettford's ear. He responds with a lazy kiss on her hand.

Her eyes meet Arthur's. They share a smile and she heads straight for him. The smile on her face is nothing compared to the grin plastered all over Arthur's.

Blake turns to the bartender. "Who's Mr. Popular?" His head motions in Pettford's direction.

"That's Pettford. He owns the place." She notices Blake's glass is empty. "You want another?"

"No. This'll do me." He drops a few crumbled bills onto the bar and exits the club.

#

Blake leans against a lamppost across the street from the club. He tosses peanuts into his mouth.

Arthur walks out of the club with a drunk Cinnamon on his arm. She's dressed like a stripper in a librarian costume.

Blake takes a picture with his phone. They don't notice him as he keeps pace with them from the other side of the street.

Half a block in front of Arthur and Cinnamon two punk rockers amble towards them. One has a green mohawk. The other has purple hair. They're covered in blood with bloodshot eyes. Spider veins cover their necks and faces.

Arthur and Cinnamon freeze when they finally see them.

The one with the purple hair vomits blood all over the sidewalk.

Blake springs into action. He takes a step into the street and freezes before he steps into the path of an SUV.

Once it's clear, he pulls out his butterfly knife and gallops to their aid.

Arthur attempts to drag Cinnamon to safety but she's too drunk. She falls to the ground and drags Arthur with her.

The punk rockers rush them.

Blake stops to allow another car to pass.

Arthur rises and attempts to help Cinnamon to her feet, but she pulls him back to the concrete.

Blake arrives and throws himself between the two men and the duo on the ground. The guy with the green mohawk lunges for Blake, but he buries his butterfly knife into his face. With his knife lodged in the green mohawk guy's face, Blake kicks the punk rocker with purple hair as he tries to get around them.

Purple hair guy rises with a hiss. Blake pulls the knife out of the other guy's face. He falls to the ground, dead. Without hesitation, Blake lunges for the purple haired rocker and drives his knife into the back of his head. Blake pulls the knife out of the dead punk rocker's skull.

Cinnamon and Arthur take in the carnage around Blake's feet. Cinnamon slurs, "Are those the crazies I've been hearing about?"

Arthur says, "Thanks, mister. You okay?"

Blake cleans the knife on his pants. "I'm fine. But be careful." He turns and rushes off in the opposite direction.

Three

Elizabeth flips through the pictures of Arthur and Cinnamon. Each new image opens her wounds a little more.

Blake sits on the corner of his desk. "I'm sorry."

Elizabeth pulls a wad of cash out of her purse. "Here's the rest of your money." She drops it onto his desk. "Thank you for your hard work."

He counts the money as Elizabeth rushes out of the office. She slams the door behind her.

Blake opens his desk drawer and pulls out a bottle of whiskey. He grabs a rock glass from the top of the cabinet, blows the dust out of it, and pours himself a drink.

The office bedroom features a DIY aesthetic. Everything is moveable and collapsible. A clothes rack functions as a closet. The bathroom has no door, only a curtain held by a crooked rod.

With his drink in hand, Blake steps into the bedroom and collapses onto the futon. He doesn't bother to take his shoes off as he stretches out. A sip of his drink is followed by an exhale.

There's a knock at the door. He ignores it and takes another sip. After the second knock, he drags himself to a sitting position and takes another sip. The third knock is enough to bring him to his feet and out of the bedroom.

Blake answers the door with his drink in hand. On the other side stands Detective Walsh. An Irish man in his late fifties dressed in a trench coat and cheap suit. Blake steps aside and the detective struts into the office.

Detective Walsh takes in the office with a cockiness he doesn't even attempt to hide. Blake closes the door and takes a seat at his desk. He eyes Walsh as he raises the glass to his lips.

Walsh is in no hurry. He takes out a pack of cigarettes and offers one to Blake.

Blake eyes it for a moment. "I quit."

Walsh lights it, takes a drag and tilts his head back and exhales the smoke into the room. "Business a little slow?"

"Something like that."

Walsh eyes the drink in Blake's hand. "Little early, ain't it?"

Blake swirls the drink around in the glass. "I've already had to tell a woman her husband is cheating on her."

"Hell of a way to earn a living."

Blake examines the drink in the glass. "What do you want, Walsh?"

Walsh takes another drag of his cigarette. "Someone's got some bad dope out on the streets. I'm sure you've seen the crazies running around."

"I've seen 'em."

Walsh continues. "The folks in the higher pay grades are saying it's gonna hit epidemic proportions if we don't get a handle on it. Mayor's putting pressure on my higher ups. Which means, they put pressure on us."

Blake says, "I'm not paid to care about those things anymore."

"I know. But I figured if anybody knew anything, it'd be you."

Blake sits back in his chair. Takes another sip of his drink. "I don't."

"You'd tell me if you did, wouldn't you?"

Blake doesn't answer.

Walsh takes another drag. Blows the smoke out in Blake's direction. "If you stumble across something, give me a call. Same number."

"You can see yourself out."

Walsh lets himself out.

#

Ouroboros is nearly empty. A petite Cambodian woman in her mid-thirties prepares an opium pipe on the floor. Her nipples poke through her green sheer nightgown. She exudes a sexy confidence despite the burn mark running up the right side of her neck. Blake makes himself comfortable on a mound of cushions. The woman puts the finishing touches on the opium pipe.

Blake leans in and whispers, "Make it a double."

She pauses. Contemplates whether to proceed.

Blake tosses a wad of cash onto her tray. "That ease your concerns?"

She hands him the pipe and says, "Take it easy. Okay?" The woman gathers her things and shuffles off.

#

A pool of blood expands on a floor. It grows as more drops fall into it.

An overturned toolbox. Its contents are all over the floor.

A man's bloody hand grips an even bloodier hammer. Blood drips off the hammer and gets absorbed into the puddle.

There's an overturned table in the corner. Pieces of broken chairs are all over the floor.

#

Blake is passed out on the cushions. His phone vibrates in his pocket. The disturbance causes him to stir. It continues to vibrate. He pulls the phone out of his pocket and answers it. "Yeah."

Whatever was said on the other side pulls him out of his malaise. He springs to his feet. "Be at my office in twenty."

Four

Blake paces the office with a drink in hand. There's a knock at the door and he rushes to answer it.

Elizabeth Preston steps into the office. Sunglasses cover her face. Her demeanor is sullen.

Blake closes the door behind her. As he turns to face her, she says, "I confronted my husband about his cheating."

With a delicate touch, Blake removes her sunglasses to reveal a black eye. Rage builds inside him.

Elizabeth says, "We got into an argument. He looks meek, but when he gets mad…" She's too distraught to finish. Tears form in her eyes. She turns away from Blake to hide her vulnerability. "I can't go back there. You don't know what he's capable of."

Blake grabs the bottle of whiskey and another glass. He pours her a drink and refills his.

Words tumble out of Elizabeth's mouth. "You have to help me, Mr. Fields. I don't have anywhere else to go."

"I'll get you a hotel room."

Elizabeth takes a step towards him with eyes full of worry and desperation. "Can't I stay here with you?"

"You don't want to stay here."

They're inches apart when she says, "I'm scared. I don't want to be alone."

Blake sips his drink.

She says, "Please. I won't be a burden. I don't have anywhere else to go."

Blake retreats until his back hits his desk. "Only for tonight. We'll figure something out."

"Thank you, Mr. Fields."

"Call me Blake."

#

Blake attempts to turn his bedroom into a livable space.

Elizabeth sits on the edge of the futon. Her eyes follow Blake as she takes a sip of her drink. "Tomorrow while he's at work, I'll go home and get a few things. I've got a sister who lives in New York. I can stay with her."

Blake crams a wrinkled shirt into a particle board dresser. "You sure it's okay for you to go back alone? I can go with you in case things go awry."

"I don't want to disrupt your other jobs. I'll be fine." She stares into her glass. "I'd been assuming there was someone else. Even prepared myself for it. Woman's intuition, you know. But once you get confirmation…" She wipes away a tear.

Blake stands in front of her. "You can have the futon. I'll sleep at my desk." He turns and heads for the door but she grabs his hand.

"I can't let you do that. We're both adult enough to share the futon." She takes another sip of her drink. "I hope I'm not being too forward."

Blackout curtains cover the lone window in the bedroom. Darkness envelops the space.

Blake and Elizabeth are asleep on opposite sides of the bed. Fully clothed. No touching.

Elizabeth stirs. She's still asleep as she positions herself so her head rests on Blake's chest.

Blake puts his arm around her.

The first rays of morning light form a yellow outline around the curtain. Blake yawns and rolls over.

Elizabeth is gone.

Startled, he pulls himself into a sitting position. On the bed next to him is a note. It reads:

YOU ARE A TRUE GENTLEMAN
THANKS XOXO

#

Blake's feet are propped on the desk as he reads the newspaper and drinks tea. The headline reads:

WOMAN EATS POODLE!!

His cell-phone rings. When he makes out who the caller is, he leaps out of his chair and answers it. "Are you okay?" He listens for a moment. "Calm down. Calm down." He grabs his keys off the desk. "Where are you?"

He grabs a scrap piece of paper and a pen and writes the address. "I'm on my way."

#

The stainless-steel refrigerator works to repel the blood on its face. White kitchen cabinets provide a neutral palette for the crimson fluid sprayed across them. Blood drips from the cabinets and onto the faux marble countertops.

Elizabeth's bare feet leave bloody footprints on the wood floor as she paces. Her blood-soaked long sleeved yellow dress matches the gruesomeness of the kitchen.

A half-packed suitcase sits in the doorway. A bloody knife sits on the kitchen table. Next to the suitcase is the decimated body of Arthur Preston. Two dozen stab wounds populate his face, torso, and stomach. Defensive wounds cover his hands and arms.

Blake leans in the doorway. Arthur's body has his full attention. "Tell me what happened. From the beginning."

Elizabeth continues to pace. She shakes out her hands. "I was packing to go to my sister's place. He came home early. I didn't know what to do. It was me and the monster." She rubs her hands together, but the blood remains. "I could see the rage in his eyes. He started yelling things about love and trust." She wipes her hands on her dress. The blood smears.

Blake maneuvers around the body and dodges the puddles of blood. He pulls the dish rag off the oven handle and runs it under the water.

Elizabeth continues. "I told him those were two things he knew nothing about. He came after me. I didn't know what to do, Blake. I promised myself never again. Never again would he put hands on me."

Blake takes her hands in his and uses the dish rag to wipe them clean.

Elizabeth continues. "I grabbed the knife. I begged him to stop. But he didn't. He didn't stop. It happened so fast. I didn't know what else to do. I was scared, Blake. Scared for my life." She collapses into Blake's arms. His shoulder muffles her words. "What are we gonna do, Blake?"

"We need to get rid of the body."

She sobs. "I'm sorry I got you involved in all this."

"Do you have any rugs? Anything big enough to wrap the body in?"

Elizabeth pulls away and composes herself. "I'm sure we've got something." She rushes out of the kitchen.

Blake kneels and inspects the body.

Arthur isn't wearing a wedding ring.

Elizabeth drags a large Persian rug into the kitchen. "Will this do?"

"Perfect." He turns his attention back to Arthur's hand. "The bastard isn't even wearing his wedding ring?

Elizabeth drops the rug on the only section of the floor not covered in blood. "He must have been with... her."

Blake takes in the kitchen. "This place needs a good cleaning. When it gets dark, we'll get the body out of here. I know a place we can get rid of it."

Five

The first quarter moon illuminates the path as Blake maneuvers his car through the darkness of nature. Dry and dying trees populate the forest and line both sides of the path. Darkness shrouds the questions lurking on the other side of visibility.

The path morphs into a clearing. Blake brings the car to a stop. He and Elizabeth get out and make their way around and pop the trunk. Inside are two shovels and Arthur's body, wrapped in the rug.

Tree roots, stones, and low visibility hamper Blake and Elizabeth's progress. They're also carrying the corpse of a 250-pound man. Blake holds Arthur under the shoulders. Elizabeth holds his feet. The two shovels sit on top of the body. A suffocating silence hangs in the air. In this place, even the insects are dead.

Blake stops. Surveys the area. "This should work."

Exhausted, Elizabeth drops her half of the body. Arthur hits the ground and decimates two dozen dry leaves. The sound of whole leaves turning into fragments pierces the air. "Sorry."

Blake ignores her as he lowers the body with respect. He grabs the two shovels and hands one to Elizabeth. There's no need for words. Blake's shovel is the first to penetrate the earth.

The ground is compact and stubborn. Unseen roots act as barriers to the lower depths of the grave they attempt to build.

They work in silence and the mound of earth grows larger. Elizabeth leans on her shovel and sucks in the night air. "We should have brought water."

Blake plunges his shovel deeper into the ground. "Sorry."

Elizabeth chuckles. "It's as much my fault as it is yours." She peers into the shallow grave. "How much further are we digging?"

Blake tosses a shovel full of dirt onto the mound. "We're about halfway." He uses the shovel to lift a stone out of the hole. "It's gotta be deep enough so some dog walker doesn't find him."

Elizabeth sighs and drives her shovel into the hole. She scoops half a shovel's worth of dirt and adds it to the mound.

A rustling sound violates the silence. Blake places a finger to his lips.

Elizabeth doesn't move.

Silence.

The rustling sound returns. This time much closer. Elizabeth whispers, "What do we do?"

Blake taps his finger against his lips, this time more forceful.

The rustling draws even closer.

Elizabeth's eyes scour the darkness.

Blake grips his shovel.

Two women emerge from the brush. One has navy blue yoga pants and a blood-covered gray hoodie. The other has black yoga pants and a red windbreaker. Both have bloodshot eyes and spider veins. They lock in on Blake and Elizabeth. Black yoga pants hisses. Blue yoga pants unloads a stream of blood-infused vomit.

Blake raises his shovel. Prepares for battle.

Elizabeth raises her shovel. Her hands quiver. She's terrified. Blake puts himself between her and the women. "Go."

The two women charge.

Elizabeth sprints in the opposite direction.

Blake drives the shovel into the chest of blue yoga pants. She falls to the ground. But black yoga pants lunges for him. He pulls the shovel out of blue yoga pants. Blood sprays his trousers. He turns and brings the shovel across the face of black yoga pants. She falls to the ground.

Blue yoga pants coughs up blood that mixes with the blood from her chest. Blake arrives and plunges the shovel through her skull, splitting her head in two.

Black yoga pants pulls herself to her feet. She's about to charge, but the head of a shovel explodes out of her stomach. She turns her bloodshot eyes downward to see her own entrails dangle off the shovel. Behind her, Elizabeth gags from the smell.

Blake swings his shovel and slices off black yoga pant's head. Elizabeth uses the shovel to push the decapitated body to the ground, opposite of where her head landed.

Elizabeth says, "This is the first time I've ever seen them in person."

Blake heads towards Arthur's body. "Let's get your husband in the ground."

#

The first rays of morning battle the black of night.

Blake drives. Elizabeth rides shotgun. Both are filthy.

Elizabeth breaks the silence when the car exits the freeway. "I hate to ask but –"

"Of course, you can."

#

Blake remains in his blood and dirt-covered pants and collared shirt. He paces with a whiskey neat in his hand. The sound of the shower fills the makeshift bedroom. He takes a sip of the drink and glances at the curtain separating the bathroom from the rest of the room.

The shower turns off. He finishes the rest of his drink and pulls a white tank top off the floor, then glances at a pile of clothes in the corner. Grabs a pair of silk boxers off the top. Sniffs them. Satisfied they don't smell; he clutches them as Elizabeth steps out of the shower. The towel hiding her body begs to be set free.

Blake says, "Sorry, I know the hot water can be finicky."

"It was fine. Thank you."

Blake makes his way past her. She steps to the side but remains so close he has to brush her on the way by.

In the shower, Blake lets the water cover his face. Blood and dirt mix with the soap and water. The drain struggles with the water and it pools in the bottom of the tub. Blake uses his toe to massage the now muddy water into the drain. His toe and the drain have his full attention. He doesn't notice Elizabeth until she steps into the shower with him.

Blake turns and is confronted by her nakedness. The water splashes his back. "You already showered."

She takes him into her hand and gently pulls him towards her wet body. "I know." Before he can respond, she crams her tongue into his mouth. He pulls her into his body and lets his hands explore her curves.

Blake groans as she massages him until he grows in her hand. He turns her around and cups her breasts. Her hands slap the wet wall as she bends over. His foot coerces her legs apart and he slides himself into her. Her warmth is wet and inviting. Each thrust gets a moan in response. Blake moves his hands to her hips. She responds with an arch of her back. Blake brings his hand to her shoulder. His body pushes against hers. She responds by driving her hips back into him.

#

Elizabeth lies in bed. Naked and wide awake. Blake snores in the spot next to her. She lets her eyes take him in. The muscular frame with the three scars on his left rib cage. Her eyes linger on his cock. Even flaccid, the size is impressive. She rolls over and grabs her phone. It's 10:53 in the morning. On her back, she scrolls through her emails.

Blake's tone is groggy. "How long have you been awake?"

She lowers the phone. "Couple of minutes." She turns her body to him so he can get a full view of her. "Should I leave town? Go to my sister's place?"

"It's gonna look suspicious."

Elizabeth closes her eyes. "I can't go about my day like nothing happened." She opens her eyes and they plead with Blake for instructions.

"Come up with an alibi," Blake says, "and go file a missing person's report this evening."

"What about you?"

Blake rubs the sleep out of his eye. "I'm going to establish my alibi for last night."

She rolls over onto her back and opens her legs slightly and runs her thumb along the crevice between her breasts. Her nipples harden. "Will I see you again?"

Blake cups her breast and lets his thumb graze over her erect nipple. "After we're in the clear, I'll make sure we see each other."

Six

Murph's Place sits in the middle of the worst section of the city. Often referred to as the beating heart of Skid Row, it's a place where misery can get a cheap meal. It features worn-out decor, worn-out cooks, worn-out waitresses, and worn-out patrons.

Alone at a booth in the back corner, Blake consumes a slice of apple pie.

Into the diner steps a man in his early thirties with a face full of scars. He looks like he was stitched together by a doctor working out of a motel. His trench coat and suit are as worn out as the rest of the place. His name is Rocks and he strolls across the diner then takes a seat across from Blake.

Blake keeps his eyes on his pie. "I know you?"

Rocks speaks as if he's got a mouth full of mashed potatoes. "Blake Fields, yeah?"

Blake takes a healthy bite of his pie. He chews like a man with nothing but time.

This agitates Rocks. He glances over his shoulder.

Finally, Blake swallows. "You a cop?"

"I hate cops."

Blake stares at his plate. "I'll take that as a no. How'd you know I'd be in here?"

The man chuckles to himself. "Call it intuition. Me, you can call Rocks." He glances around to see if anyone is paying attention. "I got a job for ya."

Blake takes a gulp of his water. "I'm off the clock."

"My boss heard you're the best, yeah."

Blake sets the now empty glass back on the table. "Who's your boss?"

Rocks growls. "If my boss wanted you to know who he was, he wouldn't have sent me. You want the job or not?"

"You haven't told me what it is."

Rocks leans in. "Guy missed a meeting yesterday. we need you to find him. Guy's name is Arthur Preston."

The mention of Arthur Preston staggers Blake. He takes in a forkful of pie to buy himself some time.

Rocks studies Blake as he chews.

Between chews, Blake says, "Sorry. Can't help you."

"Our money not good enough for you, yeah?" Rocks fidgets in his seat.

"Missing person jobs take a lot of time. Time, I don't currently have."

Rocks leans back in his chair. "Boss won't like that."

"I can recommend a few guys."

Rocks pulls himself out of the booth. Eyes narrow on Blake. "Boss ain't used to gettin' turned down. He ain't gonna be happy about this."

The last bite of pie disappears into Blake's mouth. "My sincerest apologies."

Rocks storms out of the diner.

Blake pulls out his phone and dials a number.

#

Elizabeth wears a path in the stained carpet of Blake's office. She's hysterical. "Did he mention me? Does he know what we did last night?"

Blake sits on his desk. "No. He said his boss wanted me to find Arthur Preston. You have any idea who may be looking for your husband?"

"I don't."

Blake hops off his desk and grabs Elizabeth's hand. "Who did he work for?"

"He was a scientist." Her eyes gloss with wetness. "I'm scared, Blake." She buries her head in his chest. "What's going to happen to us?"

Blake's phone rings. He pulls himself away from her and answers it. His tone is hushed. "How's it going, Theda?" He listens for a moment. "Okay. I'll be over shortly." He ends the call.

Elizabeth places her hand on his shoulder. "You okay?"

"It was a friend of mine. Go to your sister's place. Lay low."

Elizabeth takes a step back. "I'm not gonna leave you here."

"I'll be fine."

Elizabeth wipes a tear off her face. It smears her makeup. "Should I file a missing person's report before I leave?"

"No. Just get out of town."

Elizabeth grabs her purse off the cabinet. "I don't know if I'm built to handle prison."

Blake grabs her and pulls her into his body. "I won't let them haul you off." He kisses her. After a moment they disengage and Blake says, "Go home. Pack. Stay with your sister until you hear from me."

#

Roughly three miles from the edge of the city sits Theda's Auto Body Shop. A chain link fence separates the property from the rest of the city. At first glance, the shop resembles a scrap yard.

Dozens of cars sit on rusted jacks and cinder blocks. Spare parts are strewn across the lot. Piles of steering wheels and tires create a maze of rubber and metal. Mechanics in grease-covered uniforms hustle about.

Blake leans on his car by the main office. He takes a drag from a brand-new cigarette and drops it to the ground. He stubs it out with his foot.

Out steps a Puerto Rican woman with thick, curly black hair. A knife scar forms a line across her left cheek. She's covered in grease and dirt. The name tag on her jumpsuit reads "Theda". She uses a rag to clean her hands as she approaches Blake. "Blake Fields."

"Theda."

Blake notices a smudge of grease on her forehead. He points to his own forehead. "You've got some…"

She rubs the back of her hand across her forehead and examines the results. "Adds to my sex appeal, baby. Guess who came in this morning talking about you?"

"I'm in a rush, Theda."

Theda chortles. "Ain't we all." She spits and rubs it out with her boot. "Your old buddy Walsh. Came around here asking about what I was doing last night. Who I was with."

Blake stiffens. "What did you tell him?"

"Told him I was at home minding my own business. Said maybe he should try it sometime. He wasn't happy about the wisecrack. Then he says he wants to know what one of my friends was doing last night around ten." She pulls out a stick of gum. "I told him I had a lot of friends. I told him he needed to be more specific." She crams the gum in her mouth. "He says he's talkin' about Blake Fields." She studies Blake's reaction.

Blake buries his hands into the pockets of his coat.

Theda continues. "I told him, sorry buddy. I haven't seen Blake Fields in over three months."

"Thanks, Theda."

She grins. "He has the nerves to tell me if I hear anything, give him a ring. Pssst. Yeah right. Like I'm gonna rat my friend out to some cop."

"I appreciate it, Theda. Anything else?"

Theda glances around the lot. "Life is always about something else. In this case, it could be something. Could be nothing. Three weeks ago, some chick comes in here asking questions about you. Dark hair. Cute. Mentioned she was from the Times. Wanted information about how you helped me. She was doing a story. I didn't give her any info. And I never saw the story."

"Did she pitch a name?"

Theda chuckles. "She may have tossed it, but I don't remember catchin' it."

Blake turns back to his car.

Theda says, "Blake if you're into something and need help, you know I'm here for you. I owe you."

Blake turns to Theda. "You don't owe me anything, Theda."

Seven

Cinnamon and two other women perform on the stage in black and pink corsets with sequined bras. Their black ruffled skirts flow down the back of their legs. Rhinestones cover their black gloves. The choreography is seductive and trance-like.

Blake watches from the corner of the bar. He sucks down his whiskey.

Rocks takes a seat next to him. "Told you boss would be none too happy."

"Sorry to disappoint him."

Rocks watches the performance. "Interesting fact. The guy we wanted you to find used to hang out in this club. Funny, yeah?"

Blake doesn't bother to turn towards Rocks. "I guess. But I'm more into slapstick."

The joke hurdles over Rocks' head. The three women on stage turn and bend over. They pat each other's butts. Rocks licks his lips.

"What do you want, Rocks?"

Rocks sucks his teeth. "Right now, I want to know what you're doing in here."

"I was enjoying a drink and watching the girls."

Rocks finally turns to Blake. "Yeah?"

Blake meets his gaze. "Yeah."

Rocks surveys the bar to make sure nobody is paying them any attention. Satisfied with his findings, he pulls out an envelope and slides it across the bar to Blake. "Boss decided you're working for us now, yeah. Find Arthur Preston."

"What if I can't find him?"

Rocks gets out of his seat. "We'll find you." He turns and makes his way out of the club as the dancers exit the stage.

Blake stuffs the envelope into his pocket.

In the back corner sits Pettford and Mitchell. They're in the midst of a heated discussion. Pettford's two burly bouncers approach Mitchell. They motion for him to come with them.

Mitchell declines the invitation.

The bouncers take another step closer. Mitchell jumps out of his seat and back peddles away from the table and across the club. The bouncers pursue him until finally, he exits.

Blake watches the entire situation. Cinnamon, now dressed in sweats, arrives at the bar next to him. She turns to Blake and grins. Blake responds with, "Can I buy you a drink?"

Cinnamon doesn't hesitate with her drink order. Seems she never intended to buy her own drink. "Tequila my love. Straight up."

Blake motions for the bartender. "Get the lady a tequila. Straight. I'll have another." The bartender shuffles off to make the drinks.

Cinnamon leans into Blake's space. "You look familiar. What's your name handsome?"

"Blake Fields."

She extends her hand. "Cinnamon." They shake. The bartender arrives with the drinks. Cinnamon wraps her fingers around the glass. "If you came for my show, I'm afraid you missed it."

Blake takes a sip of his drink. "I saw it. You were great. But your dancing isn't why I'm here."

Cinnamon chugs her drink and motions for another.

Blake continues, "Could I have a word with you? In private."

"Sounds like my kind of party. I get off in an hour." She takes a napkin off the bar. "You got a pen?" The bartender sets her new tequila in front of her.

Blake produces a pen from the inside of his coat.

Cinnamon grabs it and scribbles. "Here's my address. come by in about two hours. We'll do all the talking you want." She kisses the napkin and drops it on the bar, dusts off her tequila and struts away.

#

Cinnamon's one-bedroom apartment is a dump. It looks like it rained laundry.

Blake stands in the middle of the apartment. His attention is on a pile of bras and panties in the corner. It's unclear if they're clean or not.

Drunk on tequila and life, Cinnamon stumbles towards the bedroom. "Make yourself a... drink. I'm going to slip into something a little more comfortable." She disappears into the bedroom and slams the door.

Blake arrives in the kitchen. He pulls a glass out of the cupboard and blows the dust out of it. A bottle of cheap whiskey sits on the counter. He opens it and gives it a sniff. The scent is strong and cheap. He peers inside the bottle. Nothing too disgusting. He pours himself a healthy drink.

Midway through a sip, he notices a cat calendar on the wall. On one of the days, it reads:

MEETING AT HOLDIN PARK NOON

Blake lowers the glass. "That's tomorrow."

Cinnamon leans on the doorframe. She's dressed in a sheer robe with nothing underneath. "Would you like to pet my pussy, Mr. Fields?"

Blake shifts his focus from the calendar to Cinnamon. "Mam, I'm gonna assume there's a cat in here somewhere."

Cinnamon giggles as she makes her way to the booze. "You gonna tell me what's so important you had to tell me in private? Or are you trying to get me alone?" She pours herself a robust drink. "Not that a guy like you needs lies to get a girl in the sack."

She doesn't bother to put the top back on the bottle. "You're the strong silent type, aren't you? Walking around, ignoring all the girls who throw themselves at you." With glass in hand, she sashays towards him. "I bet the more you ignore the ladies, the more they toss themselves at your feet. But you're too good for them. Aren't you?"

Blake sips his drink.

Cinnamon studies him from a foot away. "I know what it is. You got some sort of heartbreak in your past. Some chick who took out your heart and did a little tap dance on it before she handed it back to you all wrapped in tears and apologies."

She sips her drink and closes the distance between them. "And now you sit back and wait. With those silent stares and tough guy looks. But somewhere in there, you're just another lonely sap looking for a little action. No matter how much it costs."

"How much is it costing Arthur Preston?"

Cinnamon recoils with a giggle. Her eyes never leave Blake as she inhales her drink. "It's not costing him anything."

"I doubt that."

Cinnamon lowers her glass. Her eyes narrow. "Oh yeah?"

Blake turns his attention to the scattered clothes on the floor. "Guy like him can't get a girl like you without paying."

"Who are you," Cinnamon says. "Cupid's agent?"

"Maybe I sell him his arrows."

Cinnamon says, "How much you charging?"

"An arm and a leg." Blake finishes his drink.

"Sounds to me like you're ripping him off," Cinnamon says.

"Sounds to me like you're hiding something."

Cinnamon sets her drink on the table and makes her way to the door. She's wasted. Each step is a near tumble.

Blake attempts to hide the desperation in his tone. "What was Arthur Preston into?"

Cinnamon spins to face Blake. "Was?"

Blake breaks eye contact and covers his tracks. "I've been hired to find him. He missed a meeting. You seen him?"

"Nope."

Blake studies her. "Sure, you're not hiding something from me?"

"We're all hiding something. Even if we're hiding it from ourselves." She opens the front door. "Now, if you're not interested in playing with my…kitty, I'm going to have to ask you to leave. A girl's gotta get her beauty sleep."

Blake hands her the glass on his way out of the apartment.

Eight

Hamburgers sizzle on the griddle. The air is thick with the aroma of burnt American cheese and the grease from eighty-twenty ground beef.

Blake devours a slice of apple pie in the back booth.

A waitress arrives and puts the check on his table. "When are you gonna come in here and order something other than pie?"

"When you start serving whiskey."

With a chuckle, she leaves. On her way into the kitchen, she passes Detective Walsh. He takes a seat across from Blake. His eyes fixate on the last bite of pie on his plate.

Blake devours the last bite of pie.

Walsh finally says, "I'm working on a missing persons case. Guy named Arthur Preston. heard of him?"

With a mouthful of pie, Blake mumbles, "Doesn't ring a bell."

Walsh sits back. Eyes the diner. "Seems he contacts his mom pretty often. He's missed the last couple of calls. She's worried."

Blake sets his fork next to his plate. "I'm sure he'll appear."

Walsh leans in. "Are you sure you don't know him?"

Blake sips his water. Tries to read the weathered face of the man across from him.

Walsh continues. "I've got some witnesses; say the other night some guy saved him and a stripper from some crazies. It happened outside of the Scarlet Room. Guy they described reminded me of you."

Blake says, "Tall, dark and handsome?"

"The guy had a butterfly knife."

Blake leans back in his chair. Takes a moment to inspect his fingernails. "I was in the area. Saw they needed help. There a law against helping those in need?"

"Then you do know him." Walsh takes out his note-book. Jots some notes.

Blake inspects the nails on his other hand. "I didn't know his name. We didn't trade business cards. We're not having Sunday dinner."

Walsh continues to take notes. He doesn't take his eyes off his notebook. "What were you doing in the area?"

"I had been at the club."

Walsh glances at Blake. "Why were you there?"

"Women and whiskey."

Walsh puts his pen on the table. "You helped him and the stripper fight off some crazies. He didn't tell you his name or anything, and you left? Like some type of caped crusader?"

Blake eyes the check on the table.

"Anything else you want to tell me?"

Blake takes out cash and tosses it on the check. "If anything surfaces, I'll give you a buzz."

Walsh stands. "You do that."

#

An unidentifiable man decimates another man's face with a hammer.

A bloody butcher knife is on the floor.

Theda cowers in the corner. She uses her hand to cover the deep gash on her left cheek. Blood reddens her wrist.

Satisfied his victim is dead, the unidentifiable man stands. The light hits his face to reveal the man is Blake. He's covered in blood. Some of it is his. Most of it's not. He reaches a blood-covered hand out to Theda.

She accepts it.

#

Blake is passed out on a stack of cushions in his favorite section of Ouroboros. An opium pipe sits by his side. An empty tray sits on the floor in front of him.

Nine

Rocks sits behind the driver's seat of his pristine sedan. He uses binoculars to watch the underground entrance to Ouroboros.

Black steps out and checks his watch. He's haggard and groggy. With his hands stuffed into the pockets of his trench coat, he ventures into the alley.

Rocks lowers the binoculars and takes out his cell phone. He dials a number and waits for an answer. "He's finally leaving Ouroboros. Doesn't seem like he's looking for the guy." He squints to keep Blake in his line of sight. "Could be. Should I stay on him, yeah?"

#

Blake creeps through the woods. The trees are thick. Birds soar overhead, barely visible in the gray skies. The ground is damp from the morning drizzle.

A muffled scream disrupts the silence. Blake rushes deeper into the woods towards the sound.

Something ahead catches his attention and he freezes. Through the brush he gets a glimpse of Cinnamon. She's on the ground. Tied to a tree and gagged. Her jeans are dirty and her green blouse is torn.

Blake rushes to her and takes a knee. He works to free her from the gag and the restraints.

When the gag is out of her mouth, Cinnamon stretches her jaw. "Thank you."

Somewhere deep in the woods to the right of them, an unmistakable sound is heard. Footsteps. And they're in a hurry.

Blake helps Cinnamon to her feet.

Three people burst out of the woods and sprint towards them. Two men and a woman. All of them covered in blood.

Blake positions himself between them and Cinnamon. He whips out his butterfly knife.

The first guy is in a postal uniform. He gets sliced in the neck by Blake's butterfly knife. He gurgles and falls to the ground. Blood seeps out of the neck wound and puddles on the ground.

The second one is dressed in basketball shorts and a Michael Jordan jersey. He lunges for Blake but he rams his butterfly knife into his skull. The hole in his head makes a sucking sound as Blake pulls the knife out. He falls to his knees.

Cinnamon watches in horror as Blake wheels around and jams his knife into the woman's eye socket. He uses his foot to kick her backwards. When the knife comes out of her eye socket, blood from the hole gushes out and covers her Yale sweatshirt.

Cinnamon screams.

Postal uniform guy is on his feet. Blood spews out of its neck wound. He's stunned, but he still closes in on Cinnamon.

Blake grabs a softball-sized rock off the ground. Postal worker has his back to him. Blake seizes the opportunity. He rushes him and tackles the former postal worker.

Cinnamon sidesteps them as they plummet to the ground.

Blake pushes his face into the dirt and uses the rock to bash in the back of his head. The rock connects with his skull over and over until there's nothing left but mush.

Cinnamon turns her head and vomits.

Blake rises to his feet. Offers a bloody hand to Cinnamon. "Follow me."

She takes his hand and he leads her through the woods. Dozens of footsteps are behind them. Their pace is quick. The footsteps gain on Cinnamon and Blake.

Blake's rusted-out car appears two hundred-meters in front of them.

The sound of footsteps surrounds them.

Blake lets go of Cinnamon's hand and takes out his keys. Cinnamon is right behind him as he opens the passenger side door. She dives in.

A squad of blood-soaked crazy people burst out of the woods and surround them.

Blake hustles to the driver's side of the car. He flings the door open and hops in.

The bloodied crazy people are only feet away from the car.

Blake revs the engine and throws it in drive. A bloodied red-haired woman dives onto the hood. The car speeds off with her clinging on top. She snarls at Blake and Cinnamon. The car hits a tree root at fifty miles an hour. It knocks the woman off the hood. She plummets into the dirt as the car disappears into the brush.

#

Blake maneuvers the car through the city streets.

Cinnamon peers out the window. "You were the man who saved me and Arthur from those Crazies the other night."

Blake keeps his eyes on the road. "Who did this to you?"

"Mitchell and two of his goons."

"Why?"

Cinnamon sighs. She's already over this conversation. "Something about a formula."

Blake pulls to a stop at a red light. "What formula?"

"He said Arthur Preston was working on it. But he's never told me anything about a formula."

A chorus of gunshots from outside the car.

Cinnamon gasps. "Oh my god."

On the sidewalk, five bloodied nurses battle three uniformed officers. The officers open fire on them to keep them at bay.

Cinnamon watches in horror. "Whatever it is, it's spreading."

#

Cinnamon's apartment is even messier now than it was before. The laundry piles are taller. Empty bowls are scattered across the table. Some still have traces of multi-colored cereal in them. An ashtray full of marijuana stems sits next to a lava lamp on the side table.

In the kitchen, Cinnamon pours two drinks. Straight tequila. She drinks one of them and refills it. She eyes the half-full glasses for a moment. Lost in thought until it flees and she carries the drinks across the apartment and hands one to Blake. He accepts it and positions himself in the middle of the room.

He sniffs the tequila. "Who does Arthur Preston work for?"

Cinnamon chugs half of her drink then sashays to the window and peers out. "Word is, someone's got some bad junk out on the streets. They say first you get a fever and cough up blood. Then you see stuff. After that, you can feel yourself decaying. About seven hours later, you're another crazy person running around trying to eat people." She takes another gulp. "It sounds awful. I swear, I'll kill myself before I become one of those things."

"Arthur Preston. Who does he work for?"

Cinnamon ignores the question and heads back into the kitchen. She pours herself another drink. "You tell me something first." She whirls around. Tequila sloshes out the top of her glass. "What were you doing out at that park today? Going to feed the ducks? Ha! I doubt it. You don't look like the duck-lovin' type."

Blake barks, "Who is Mitchell? How do you know him?"

Cinnamon ignores the question. "You were following me. Weren't you? You're obsessed with me, aren't you?"

"I was following you. Satisfied? Now. Who is Mitchell and how do you know him?"

Cinnamon takes another sip. "Why were you following me? Were you... stalking me?"

Blake takes a step closer to her. "My turn. Then, if you don't pass out, I'll tell you anything you want to know."

Cinnamon takes another sip. Mulls over the offer. "Mitchell's a dealer. Hangs out at the club a lot. Few days ago, he tells me he wants to meet me at the park. Said it was important."

Blake takes a healthy sip of his drink. Grimaces from the cheapness. "This formula is it –"

"I already told you. I don't know nothing about no formula. Why does everybody keep asking me about this thing?" She's about a sip away from being full-blown wasted.

Blake says, "Who's paying you to get close to Arthur Preston?"

"I'm not a whore."

Blake closes in on her. "Tell me why you were spending time with him if it wasn't for money."

Cinnamon finishes the rest of her drink. "Is that why you saved me? Give you a chance to insult me and call me names? Because if that's the case, I'd rather you left me there to die."

"Is Pettford paying you to get close to Arthur?"

Cinnamon bellows. "Will that make you happy? Fine. Pettford's paying me. I'm a little whore. Shout it from the rooftops. Cinnamon is a little whore. You happy now?" She turns to make another drink but Blake grabs her arm and spins her around.

He takes the glass out of her hand. "Enough with the liquid diet." He puts the glass on the table and heads to the front door. "Take a shower and get yourself sober."

Ten

The Scarlet Room is alive and popping. Burlesque Dancers perform on stage. Patrons drink and socialize.

Blake weaves his way through the crowd until he arrives at a table with a bevy of beautiful women. Amongst them sits Pettford. He welcomes Blake with a smirk and a raised eyebrow. The two-hundred-and-fifty-pound bouncer behind him stiffens.

Blake leans in for emphasis. "I'm gonna say a name. You tell me what pops in your head."

The bouncer's hulking mass comes around the table. Blake doesn't flinch.

Pettford stops the bouncer with a wave of his hand. "This may be interesting."

Blake's eyes stay trained on Pettford. "Arthur Preston."

Pettford grins. Relishes in the dramatic pause. Finally, the word oozes out of his mouth. "Lonely."

"What else?"

"Loyal."

The muscles in Blake's neck tense. "Loyal to who?"

Pettford chuckles. "To this club and all it has to offer. Please. Do sit. Let's discuss what's on your mind, mister…"

Blake takes a seat across from Pettford. "Blake Fields."

"And tell me Mr. Fields, why are you so interested in Mr. Preston?"

Blake eyes the bouncer. "I'm working on a case. It involves him."

"Is it a missing persons case? He hasn't been in here for a few days. Some of the ladies are worried about paying rent."

The ladies snicker as they sip their colorful cocktails.

Blake shifts his focus from the bouncer to Pettford. "Like Cinnamon?"

Pettford nestles into the neck of a blue-haired buxom woman with brown skin and a pink bra. "It's no secret she has a soft spot for him. Is this the gambit? You want information on Preston and Cinnamon?"

"It's one of the reasons. I'm also looking for a man named Mitchell."

Pettford sits back. Feigns amusement. "What would you want with the little weasel?"

"Part of the case I'm working on. Something to do with a formula."

Pettford struggles to hide his shock. "Formula? And you believe he has it?"

"I intend to find out."

Pettford pulls out a pen and scribbles something onto a napkin. He teases it in front of Blake's face. "This is Mitchell's address. you tell me who hired you, and it's yours."

Blake mulls it over. Finally, he says, "I was hired by Arthur Preston's wife."

Pettford hands the napkin to Blake.

As Blake stands, Pettford says, "Mr. Fields, you should know that Arthur Preston doesn't have a wife. Why else would he spend so much time here?"

Blake glares at Pettford and all his laughing women. Anger and embarrassment seep through his pores. He turns and marches back through the club.

Pettford yells, "Give Mitchell my best when you see him."

#

Blake knocks on the door to Mitchell's apartment. In his hand is a brown kraft envelope, folded in half.

From inside the apartment, Mitchell yells, "Who is it?"

"An old friend sent me." The chain lock keeps the door from opening too wide. Mitchell peers through the crack and gives Blake the once over.

Blake raises the envelope.

Mitchell slams the door shut. Six different locks are unlocked in rapid succession. He opens the door and motions for Blake to enter. As he steps into the apartment, Mitchell asks. "Who sent you here?"

"You'll know when you see the contents of this enve-lope. He hands it to Mitchell.

Mitchell opens it and peers inside. It's full of crum-pled newspapers. "What the –" His eyes turn upwards as he gets punched in the face. He falls to the floor. Unconscious.

#

Mitchell awakens and finds himself tied to a chair with his shirt off in the middle of the living room.

Blake enters the room. In his hands is a leather belt. He folds it into a loop as he approaches Mitchell. "I recognize you from the club. You had an argument with Pettford."

Mitchell squirms. "He the one who sent you?"

Blake studies him.

Mitchell says, "It was Breezer, wasn't it?"

"Who the hell is Breezer?" Blake pulls on both ends of the belt. The crack from the leather snaps Mitchell to attention.

Mitchell grows more desperate. "Was it Pettford or Breezer?"

"I asked you a question."

Mitchell's face has a sheen from all the sweat. Snot pours out of his nose. "Breezer's my old partner."

"What happened?"

Mitchell wriggles. "Doesn't matter."

Blake whips him across the chest with the belt. "If I ask, it matters."

Mitchell whimpers. A red streak forms across his bare chest. A drop of blood escapes from a fleck of broken skin. "Pettford wanted me for a job. But he didn't want Breezer involved."

"Why not?"

Mitchell glances at his chest. "Breezer has a temper. Him and Pettford had a falling out years ago."

"Where can I find this Breezer?"

Mitchell blurts out through the pain, "He lives with his girlfriend. 1156 River View Lane. Number 322."

Blake rummages through a stack of papers on the table until he finds something suitable to write on. He writes the address.

Outside on the street. A crowd roars.

Mitchell is frantic. 'What the hell?"

Blake races to the window and peers out. "Protestors." He turns to Mitchell. "Tell me about the formula."

"I don't know about any formula."

Blake whips him again, in the same spot. "Why did you ask Cinnamon about it?" A gash opens on Mitchell's chest. Blood flows out of the wound.

"I don't know what you're –"

There's a knock at the door.

Blake gets eye level with Mitchell. "You expecting someone?"

Mitchell shakes his head, *no*.

Another knock. This one with the thud of impatience.

Blake drags Mitchell, chair and all, into the bedroom.

The bedroom is sparse. A bed. A dresser. A nightstand with no lamp. The carpet is filthy and the wall has a calendar featuring a naked woman straddling a skateboard.

Blake delivers Mitchell next to the bed. He takes off Mitchell's sock and uses it to gag him.

Another, even more forceful knock.

Blake rushes out and closes the bedroom door behind him. He bounds across the main room and composes himself as he opens the front door.

On the other side is Alexia. A hardened criminal with her silver hair in an undercut hairstyle. She points a revolver at Blake as she enters the apartment.

Behind her, Vic enters. A monster of a man in his twenties with a face and neck full of tats.

Alexia says, "Why are you answering Mitchell's door?"

"Why are you knocking on it?" replies Blake.

Alexia keeps her eyes and the gun trained on Blake. "This one's got stones."

Vic says, "Yeah he does."

Alexia takes in the apartment. "How about you tell us where Mitchell is?"

Blake doesn't respond.

Outside, the crowd cheers.

Vic says, "I'll check the back." He heads to the bedroom.

Alexia moves the gun so it's pointed at Blake's mouth. "What business do you have with Mitchell?"

Blake says, "I'm looking for a guy named Breezer. Heard of him?"

Vic rushes out of the bedroom. "He's in the bedroom. Tied to a chair with a sock in his mouth."

Alexia says, "You know what to do."

Vic pulls out a hunting knife and disappears back into the bedroom.

The crowd outside grows even more boisterous.

Blake says, "You gonna answer my question?"

"I haven't decided yet."

From the bedroom, Vic asks, "Do you have the formula?"

Mitchell whimpers, "I don't know what you're talking about, man." The repeated sounds of a fist hitting wet flesh explodes out of the bedroom.

Vic yells, "Where is it? Tell me."

Mitchell's words bubble out of his toothless mouth. "I have no idea."

The echoes of decimation don't faze Alexia in the slightest. "I'm curious. Why Breezer?"

Vic shouts, "Anything you want to tell me? Don't make me use this."

Blake says, "Job I'm working on."

The words tumble out of Mitchell's mouth in mushed slurs. "There's this girl. Works for Pettford. Her name's Cinnamon. She may know. That's all I got. I swear."

Vic speaks between gulps of air. "I need you to give me something else."

Alexia raises the gun so it's at eye level with Blake. "For who?"

Blake says, "Can't tell you."

Mitchell's words are barely audible. "I'm not lying...
you, I'd tell you, if...I knew... more." His muffled screams
drown out the low hum of the crowd outside... until they
don't.

Alexia grins. "What to do with you?"

Vic returns. He's covered in blood and sweat. The
knife is only covered in blood. "It's done. He claims some
girl named Cinnamon may have some information for
us." He washes the blood off the knife in the kitchen sink.

Alexia keeps her attention on Blake. "Guy here says
he's looking for Breezer. What should we do with him?"

Vic lathers a sponge with soap and water. "Kill him.
He's a witness. If he goes to the cops –"

Blake interjects. "I'm not gonna go to the cops."

Alexia snickers. "And we're supposed to believe you?"

Blake shifts his gaze to Vic, who has his back to him.
"You'll have to trust me."

Vic laughs.

Alexia says, "This job of yours. What's Breezer got to
do with it?"

When Blake doesn't answer, Alexia puts the gun
against his forehead.

Vic uses a striped dish rag to dry the knife.

Blake says, "All I can tell you is; it involves the
formula."

Vic freezes.

Alexia says, "What about the formula?"

Blake says, "I have it."

Alexia moves the gun off of Blake's forehead. "Where?"

Blake glances over his shoulder. Satisfied Vic isn't close enough to do any damage, he turns back to Alexia. "I don't talk to underlings."

Alexia and Vic exchange a look and Alexia says, "You're coming with us."

Vic opens the door. Alexia shoves the gun into Blake's back, pushing him out the door.

Eleven

Outside of Mitchell's apartment building, the streets are total bedlam. Protestors stand shoulder to shoulder. Many of them hold signs reading things such as:

DON'T KILL ADDICTS! HELP THEM!
DON'T TRUST THE GOVERNMENT
DEATH TO THE 1%
STOP THE MAN MADE PLAGUE

A black woman with dreads and doorknocker earrings stands on top of a minivan. Her camouflage jacket is as militant as her demeanor. She screams into a megaphone. "Are we going to watch while those who need help for their addictions are killed off?"

Vic and Alexia are behind Blake as they step into the madness. Alexia keeps her gun in her pocket and against Blake's back.

The crowd yells. "Hell no!"

The woman on the minivan works to whip her acolytes into a frenzy. "Why is it when the poison hits our community, they call us crackheads and let us die in the streets? But when it hits their communities, it's a crisis and they need help? Are our loved ones crackheads?"

The crowd replies. "Hell no!"

The woman on the minivan raises a fist in the air. "Does our community deserve respect? Do our loved ones deserve dignity? Do our loved ones deserve treatment?"

The crowd yells. "Yes, yes, yes!"

"On this day, let our voices be heard! What do we want?"

The crowd replies in unison. "A cure!"

A group of riot police in full gear, arrive a quarter block from the protestors. They get in formation and bang on their shields. The cacophony of sound is rhythmic and deafening.

This fuels the tension. The protestors aim their fury at the riot police. "A cure! A cure! A cure!"

The riot police remain in formation as they march towards the protestors.

Protestors cry out, "A cure! A cure! A cure!"

A black protestor with a huge afro and a beard bumps into Alexia. Blake seizes his opportunity. He darts between two female protestors.

Vic chases Blake into the crowd.

Alexia pushes the protestor with the afro.

The woman on the minivan continues to shout. "When do we want it?"

"Now!" barks the crowd.

The riot police close in on the crowd.

Blake dodges protestors as he tries to lose Alexia and Vic.

The riot police launch tear gas canisters into the gathered crowd.

The protest leader directs her rhetoric at the riot police. "What do we want!"

The grenades explode. Tear gas fills the air.

Blake covers his face as he tries to get out of the melee.

"A cure!" The shouts ring out and are accompanied by coughs and gags.

A protester tosses a Molotov cocktail into the riot police. It explodes. Two officers are engulfed in flames.

Chaos ensues.

The riot police rush the protestors. Batons are swung. Rubber bullets are fired. More tear gas fills the air.

The protest leader is undeterred. "When do we want it?"

The crowd remains defiant. "Now!"

Some protestors run for cover. Others stay and battle the riot police. Smoke from the tear gas envelops everything in a gray haze. Protest signs and batons clash like medieval swords.

As the battle rages on between the protestors and the riot police, other sounds join the chorus.

Screams. Growls. Hisses.

Blake's eyes are bloodshot. He wipes them with the back of his hand. Somebody runs by and bumps him. Screams and growls are all around him. He flails until he finally gains some sight.

A man with a high-top fade emerges from within the mist. A chunk is bitten out of his face, right under his left eye. A one-armed crazy grabs him around the throat and pulls him back into the mist.

Blake spins. Unable to see more than a few feet in front of his face. All around him are cries of agony. A female crazy with clumps of missing hair charges him. He whips out his butterfly knife. In a series of fluid motions, he dodges his attacker and slices her throat.

The crazy hits the ground. Blood bubbles from her mouth and neck gash.

Blake inches forward. Someone screams from only a few feet in front of him. He rushes into the mist towards a brown-haired white woman with a bloodied bodybuilder on top of her. She keeps him at bay with a protest sign against his neck.

Blake tackles the bodybuilder and gets on top of him, then snatches the protest sign from the woman and uses it to impale the bodybuilder in the middle of his face. The bodybuilder dies instantly.

Blake rises and extends his hand to the brown-haired woman. She reaches for it but three pairs of bloodied hands pull her back into the mist. Her screams are replaced by chewing sounds. Gunshots ring out. He heads in the opposite direction of the sound. Deeper into the mist. His eyes are red from the tear gas. He coughs as he goes.

Protestors scurry about. Bruised and bloodied.

A member of the riot police beats a protester with his baton. A handless crazy tackles him. Blake slips by them as the handless crazy munches on the officer's face.

The effects of the tear gas on Blake are evident. Watery eyes, trouble breathing, and excessive saliva. He ducks into an alleyway. His face is puffy as he scans the area until his eyes land on a door by a loading dock. He rushes to it and turns the knob.

It opens.

#

The door leads into an old-fashioned Italian restaurant. Complete with red and white checkerboard tablecloths and dim lighting.

Blake enters and across the dining room, the front door leads out into the city. He makes his way over and peers out the window. This side of the block is devoid of tear gas. He steps out of the restaurant and takes in the carnage.

Sounds from the battle echo in the distance. Cries for help reverberate off the buildings.

A woman cries out, "Malcolm, where are you?"

Random protesters pour water on each other's faces. A cab driver empties a bottle of water on a woman's face.

Blake arrives next to them and points to the bottle of water. "You got another one of those?" The cab driver grabs another bottle and hands it to Blake. "Thank you." As Blake dumps the water onto his face and eyes, "You taking fares?"

"I was going to get this young lady out of here."

Blake rubs the water off his face. His eyes are already getting better. "Great. We can share the cab. But we gotta go. Now."

The cab driver and the female protestor share a glance.

"I'll pay for your fare." Blake pulls out some crumbled cash.

#

Blake hops out of the cab and sprints between cars as he crosses the busy intersection. He makes his way to a dilapidated apartment building.

Inside, the building is even worse than the outside. Blake arrives at a door with peeling paint. He knocks on it.

No answer.

He knocks again.

Still, no answer.

He tries the doorknob. It's unlocked. He steps into the apartment. The carpet is clean except for Breezer's dead body sprawled on the floor. His throat is slashed open. His brown skin sags and is peppered with gray splotches. The pool of blood around his head has dried to create a large black circle in the carpet. The body started to decompose days ago.

Blake gags and uses the back of his hand to cover his nose. A dust rag sits on top of the table. He grabs it and uses it to finger a picture of Breezer and Elizabeth Preston. But her hair isn't blonde. It's brown. She's got her arms locked around Breezer. Blake returns the picture and surveys the room.

There's a stack of mail on the end table. He uses the rag to go through it. Numerous letters are addressed to Lorraine Nathanson. The realization hits him like a brick to the face.

Twelve

The Scarlet Room is closed. The bartender cleans the bar. The bouncer sweeps the floor. Pettford reads spreadsheets at the bar.

There's a knock at the door. Pettford says, "See who it is."

The bouncer goes to answer the door and Blake pushes his way in. "Where's your boss?"

Pettford turns to him with a grin. "Did you find Mrs. Preston?" He laughs.

The bouncer follows Blake to the bar. "Where can I find Lorraine?"

Pettford turns back to his spreadsheets. "I don't know who you're talking about."

"Breezer's girlfriend. Where is she?"

Pettford flips through his paperwork. "I have no idea." He motions for the bartender. "Pour this man a

healthy drink. Something tells me he's had a rough night."
Pettford studies Blake. "You look like a whiskey man." He
keeps his eyes on Blake as he says, "Make it a whiskey."

The bartender heads off to make the drink at the
opposite end of the bar.

Blake cracks his knuckles. "Well?"

"I'm not a big Breezer fan. I don't know anything
about him or his girlfriend. I know he's a hothead. I'm
sure Mitchell informed you."

Blake glances over his shoulder at the bouncer. "Yeah.
he did. Right before he was killed."

The bartender sets a whiskey neat on the bar in front
of Blake.

Pettford raises his own drink to his lips. "Mitchell's
dead? Too bad."

"He was killed while I was over there."

Pettford laughs. "Some guys have all the luck."

Blake grabs his glass. Sniffs it. "You sent those two
men to kill me and Mitchell, didn't you?"

Pettford chuckles. It's condescending. "I appreciate
your enthusiasm, but you give me way too much credit. I
run a club. I'm not the type who puts out hits. But, your
imagination is impressive. Let us toast to your creativity."
He raises his glass and smirks.

They touch glasses and sip their respective drinks.

Blake is the first to lower his glass. "If it's not you,
who wanted me and Mitchell dead?"

"Maybe they only wanted Mitchell dead." Pettford says,
"Could be you were at the wrong place at the wrong time."

Blake rubs his eyes. "Story of my life, but I don't –" he sways. His vision doubles. His eyes focus on his glass.

Pettford says, "Everything alright?"

The cup drops from Blake's hand and shatters onto the floor. Blake tries to steady himself against the bar, but it's no use. He collapses to the floor.

Pettford turns back to his spreadsheets. "Call Rocks. Tell him he can come get Fields."

#

In the deep recesses of an industrial building, Blake is strapped to a gurney, unconscious.

Three men watch him. One of them is Rocks. His face full of fury as he paces.

A doctor hovers over Blake. Even at the age of fifty-five, his unbridled joy is evident. His salt-and-pepper hair is pulled back into a ponytail. His Japanese features are bright and alert.

Next to him stands a pale-skinned red-haired man whose stomach hides his belt buckle. This is Shaunassy. He furrows his brow as the doctor whispers into his ear. He cuts off the doctor with a wave of his hand. "Administer the drug."

The doctor pulls out a comically long syringe full of milky liquid. He gives the side of it a tap with his finger and sticks it into Blake's arm.

Blake stirs. His eyelids pull apart and search the room.

Shaunassy says, "Mr. Fields. Where is Arthur Preston?"

Blake's syllables are hardly audible. "He's… he's de..ad."

Rocks loses his mind. "You kill him? That why you didn't want the job, yeah?"

Shaunassy admonishes Rocks with a wave of the hand. "Please Rocks. I'm not concerned with the murder of Arthur Preston. I want my formula."

Blake coughs. "Form..ula"

Shaunassy leans in. His excitement bubbles to the surface. "Yes. Yes. Yes. Who has it? Who has my formula?"

Blake doesn't answer.

Shaunassy shakes the gurney. "Answer me. Is it the person who killed Arthur Preston?"

"I don't… know."

The doctor whispers something else into Shaunassy's ear. He responds to the doctor's comment by folding his arms across his chest. "You're right." Shaunassy turns to Rocks. "Get him out of here. He'll be a crazy soon enough. Leave him in the back of Pettford's club. Teach the prick a lesson about wasting my time."

Blake passes out.

Thirteen

Rain falls from the early morning skies in horizontal sheets.

In the alley behind the Scarlet Room, Cinnamon kneels next to Blake. She's dressed in oversized sweatpants and a t-shirt. She's sopping wet. She slaps Blake to wake him.

He doesn't move. She slaps him again.

He comes around and pushes her away so he has room to turn his head and vomit foamy blood. When he's done, she slips his arm around her shoulders and uses her strength to help him stand.

They exit the alley. Cinnamon drags him along the street. "You okay, Blake?"

He grumbles a reply.

"Did Pettford do this to you?"

He mumbles another reply.

Behind them, someone hisses. Cinnamon turns. Half a block away from them is a teenage emo kid in a Death Cab for Cutie shirt. He's closing on them fast.

Cinnamon clocks the approaching emo kid. There's no outrunning him with Blake draped on her. She lowers him to the ground and steals a glance at the blood-covered emo kid.

Yep. He's getting closer.

Cinnamon digs around in Blake's pockets until she pulls out his butterfly knife. A glance at the emo kid.

He's within a hundred meters of her.

Cinnamon stands. Readies herself. Closes her eyes for a silent prayer.

Blake watches from the ground. He tries to speak but only produces more mumbling.

With the knife in hand, she charges the bloody emo kid.

Blake passes out.

Cinnamon screams.

#

Blake wakes on Cinnamon's couch. His coat is off and he's covered in blood. It takes him a moment to orientate himself. When he does, he pulls himself to his feet and checks his arm. Spider veins grow from the spot where the needle was injected. They spread across his arm. He sighs.

Across the room, his coat is on the floor. From the coat, a trail of blood leads to the back of the apartment. He grabs his coat and follows the trail.

The primary bathroom is cluttered and feminine. Blake stumbles into the room and finds himself face-to-face with Cinnamon. She's naked in a tub of pink water. Air gets sucked in between her lips. A chunk has been bitten out of her shoulder. Her wrists are slit.

Blake's butterfly knife sits on top of the toilet.

She turns to Blake and beams. "I killed it, Blake. I used your knife."

"What happened?"

Cinnamon coughs and blood splatters the white tile. It oozes between her breasts and finds its way into the pink water. "I saved you from the crazy. It bit me. But I killed it."

Blake examines the knife. Takes in her wrists.

She follows his eyeline to her wrists. "I heard if they bite you, you'll turn into one of them. I told you what I'd do before I let that happen."

"Cinnamon –"

She continues. "Arthur Preston treats me like… like a person. Not some piece of ass."

Blake studies her. "You telling me the truth?"

She smiles. "We're even, Blake. You saved me. I saved you. Told you I had a heart of gold."

"Technically, I saved you twice." He forces a grin.

"Minor details."

Blake kneels so he's at eye level with her. "Thank you, Cinnamon."

Cinnamon says, "Can I ask a favor?"

"Of course."

She uses her head to motion to his butterfly knife. "Could you help me along?"

"Of course." He leans over and uses the knife to slit her throat. Blood pours out of the gash and darkens the pink water.

#

Blake drags himself along the wall in the hall of his office building. He gags and uses the wall to steady himself. The urge to spew is strong, but he holds it off. His office door is only a dozen feet away.

He wills himself towards his destination and pulls the keys out of his pocket and drops them. He leans over to retrieve them and rests his head against the door before he gets the key into it.

One step into the office and he flips on the light. The LEDs flicker to life and reveal Alexia, seated with her feet on the desk. Gun pointed at Blake. "You look like shit."

The voice startles Blake but he suppresses it. "I feel even worse." He peers at the doorknob and back at Alexia. "If it wasn't my place, I'd be impressed."

"You're still impressed."

"Maybe a little." Blake makes his way to the desk and takes a seat across from her.

Alexia says, "Don't get comfortable. You're going to meet someone important."

"Is this about the formula?"

She leans on the desk. "What else would it be about?"

"I've had a long night. Reach in the top drawer. Hand me the bottle."

Alexia does as instructed and pulls out the whiskey bottle. She hands it to Blake, but never takes her eyes off him.

Blake takes a huge gulp straight out of the bottle. He offers some to her, but she declines.

Instead, she keeps her eyes and gun on Blake as she takes out her cell-phone. She hits two buttons and speaks into the phone. "Bring the car around."

Blake chugs his whiskey.

#

The customized navy-blue SUV weaves its way through the busy city streets. Its platinum rims and gold trim give the vehicle a gaudy exterior proving money can't buy taste.

Vic drives. Alexia faces Blake with her gun pointed at him.

Beads of sweat streak Blake's face. "You can't turn on the damn AC?"

Alexia laughs. "It is on."

Vic uses the rearview mirror to steal a glance at Blake. "Full blast."

Blake wipes sweat from his brow.

Alexia studies him. "How did you get your hands on the formula?"

Blake turns his attention to the world outside his window. "Hard work. A little luck."

"Why don't I believe you?"

Blake sighs. "Could be the sweat."

#

Sun rays brighten the docks and water. Expensive yachts occupy the slips. The water is tranquil. The gentle bob of the yachts in the water is melodic and meditative. A gull dive bombs the water but fails to snare a meal.

Vic leads them along the dock. Alexia uses her gun to prod Blake forward until he rushes to the side of the dock and vomits into the water.

Alexia is disgusted. "What's wrong with you?"

Blake uses the back of his sleeve to wipe his mouth. "Bad shrimp."

They continue along until they're in front of a gaudy monstrosity of a yacht. On the stern, it reads "Poseidon's Widow".

Vic is the first to arrive on the yacht. Blake and Alexia are right behind him.

Blake braces himself on the rail. He's ready to pass out.

Confined to a wheelchair on the opposite side of the deck is a woman with a patch over her left eye. Her wrinkled white skin sags. The sixty-two-year-old woman goes by Miss Isaacson and she's the definition of tacky opulence. She sips champagne as she peers over the side of the yacht. Her gold necklaces, bracelets, and rings shimmer in the sunlight.

Across from her, a beautiful, naked, brown-haired mermaid eats grapes. Her green skin shimmers in the morning light. Yellow scales cover the lower half of her body.

Blake can't take his eyes off her.

Miss Isaacson doesn't even bother to face her visitors. 'Blake Fields, I presume." Vic rushes to her chair and spins her around to face Blake and Alexia. "You can call me Miss Isaacson."

The mermaid uses her tongue to coerce a grape into her mouth.

Blake keeps his eyes on the mermaid even as he speaks to the woman in the wheelchair. "Are you the one who hired the dancer?"

Miss Isaacson glances from Vic to Alexia with a face full of confusion. "Dancer?"

Blake rips his eyes off the mermaid and focuses them on Miss Isaacson. "Her name was Cinnamon and I'm thinking you hired her to get close to Arthur Preston."

Miss Isaacson is perplexed. "I've never heard of this girl. Did you say her name was…Cinnamon?"

"Yeah. Like the spice." Blake says, "She worked at Pettford's club."

Patience dissipates and Miss Isaacson snaps, "Who the hell is Pettford?"

"I told you. He owns the club Cinnamon worked at."

Miss Isaacson uses her one good eye to assess Blake. "I'm sorry. But I'm very particular about where I go dancing." She grins. Daring him to laugh.

Blake remains stoic. He returns the stare. "Why am I here?"

Miss Isaacson chuckles. "You remind me of my third husband. Handsome. Arrogant. Stupid."

The mermaid tosses a grape into her mouth. Blake tries to stay focused on the woman with the eye patch.

Miss Isaacson says, "I've figured out all the other pieces, but you, Mr. Fields, remain a mystery."

"I hate to tell you this, but I don't know where I fit into all this either."

Alexia steps forward but keeps her gun on Blake. "He's still claiming he has the formula."

Miss Isaacson turns to Vic. "Bring her."

Vic heads below deck.

Miss Isaacson sips her champagne.

The mermaid smiles at Blake and pinches her already erect nipples. He responds by turning his eyes to the spot on his arm where the injection took place. The spider veins have doubled in length.

Alexia notices Blake's arm. "You've been given the drug, haven't you?

Blake responds with an ice-cold glare.

From below deck, Elizabeth Preston emerges. Her blonde hair is now a chestnut brown. Her hands are bound with duct tape. Her black eye is nearly healed. Vic is right behind her. She locks eyes with Blake.

Neither shows their hand to the other.

Miss Isaacson takes a moment to see how they regard each other. Finally, she says, "Lorraine here claims she has the formula. Imagine my surprise when Alexia informed me Mr. Fields is claiming to have it. Alexia my dear, there appears to be a liar in our midst."

Lorrain steps forward. "Neither of us is lying. We're working together. It was a miscommunication on our part. We have the formula. No one is lying to you, Miss Isaacson. Isn't that right, Blake?"

Blake glares at Lorraine. "It's true. Lorraine would never lie to someone about business. Nor would I."

Lorraine can't meet Blake's gaze.

Miss Isaacson shifts her one-eyed gaze from Blake to Lorraine, and back to Blake. "You're not trying to make a fool out of me, are you?"

Lorrain raises her bound hands until they are level with her chest. "Of course not. We're here to make a deal."

Miss Isaacson turns to Blake and smiles. "Quite the business partner you have here. Firm and to the point."

Blake stares at Lorraine. "Yeah. She's something else."

Lorraine is desperate to keep the focus on business. "We want three."

Miss Isaacson keeps her eye on Lorraine as she sips her champagne. When she finally lowers the glass, she says, "The absurdity."

Lorraine feigns confidence. "Is it? The longer we wait, the higher the demand. How about I – we, wait until this thing becomes a full-blown epidemic –"

"One point five." The three words are spat out like a curse.

"I could give Shaunassy a call." Lorraine's confidence grows. "After all –"

Miss Isaacson has had enough. "Two."

Lorraine pushes back. "Two point six."

Miss Isaacson softens her tone. "The longer we delay, the more people die."

Lorraine doesn't flinch. "Not my problem."

Blake barks, "For god's sake."

Lorraine is unfazed. "Two point three."

Miss Isaacson glances from Lorraine to Blake. "Done."

Lorraine motions for Vic to free her hands. "We'll get the formula and bring it back to you in three hours. Have the money ready."

Fourteen

Blake rummages through the drawers in his desk. Sweat adheres his shirt to his body. Finally, he pulls out a half-full bottle of whiskey.

Lorraine watches him from the other side of the office. "Who did this to you?"

Blake drinks half the remaining whiskey and grimaces. "Metaphorically, you did. Literally, an obese man and a doctor."

"Shaunassy?"

He finishes the last of the bottle. Tosses it at the trash can. Misses. The bottle bounces off the trash can and lands on the floor. He goes to grab it, but nearly falls. Instead, he eases himself into a chair.

Lorraine rushes to his aid.

He swats her away. "Get away from me."

She backpedals, startled by his aggression.

Blake pulls the shirt off of his skin. "How was New York?"

"You need help."

Blake coughs. "I need answers."

"Once we get the formula."

Blake pounds the desk. "I'm a dead man decaying. You didn't do it to me, but you dug the grave. Least you can do is tell me what I'm falling apart for."

She seizes the whiskey bottle. "Shaunassy went to Pettford and asked him if he knew any dealers who could put a new drug on the streets. Pettford got Mitchell." She sets the bottle on the desk. "Mitchell and Breezer were partners. Had been for years. But Pettford and Breezer didn't get along. Mitchell cut him out. Of course, the new drug is what's turning everyone crazy." She takes a step towards Blake. "Shaunassy had already hired Arthur Preston to – "

"Develop the drug and the cure. Sell the drug, make money. Get people sick. Turn around and sell the cure. Make more money. Become a hero."

Lorraine paces the room. "Having a bunch of dope fiends running around the city would collapse the property values. Once the market hits bottom, Shaunassy wants to come through and purchase the entire area. Once he owns it all, he'll release the cure."

Blake closes his eyes. "He'd make a fortune."

Lorraine turns to face Blake. "Breezer was still raw about being cut out. He decided we should take the formula and create a bidding war. It was all Breezer's idea."

"What about the girl, Cinnamon?"

Lorraine takes a moment to study Blake before answering. "We wanted you to follow her. Find out who she was working for. If anybody."

Blake stands, but he has to use the desk to steady himself. 'There's a chance nobody paid her? She genuinely liked Arthur Preston?"

Lorraine crosses her arms over her chest. "These snobby white folks are gonna get rich off people like us. They're gonna destroy our community. They're gonna kill us off and make millions. What's wrong if a couple of us find a way to profit off it? We deserve a cut."

Blake bellows, "You may have gotten an innocent girl killed."

"Any collateral damage is on Breezer. Not –"

Blake finds the strength to stand on his own. "You found out about what I did for Theda. Decided I'd be the perfect fall guy."

Lorrain turns her head to avoid eye contact.

Blake continues. "You posed as a reporter to get information on me. Right?"

Tears form in the corners of Lorraine's eyes. "Couple years ago, Breezer heard about what you did. He figured you'd be a perfect frame-up for Arthur Preston's murder. All we had to do was make it look like he roughed me up."

Blake takes an uneasy step forward. "You got greedy and killed Breezer."

"I killed him in self-defense. He would have killed me, Blake. You gotta believe me." She rushes over and lowers Blake back into his chair. "It was him or me." She sits on the edge of the desk.

Blake says, "You throw around the term "*Self-defense*" like a hand grenade."

"You believe me don't you, Blake?"

Blake gazes into her eyes. "I believe I've got about two hours until my veins pop out and I try to eat the closest person to me. I believe you were ready to sell the formula and skip town but I ruined your –"

In one quick motion, Lorraine grabs the empty whiskey bottle and smashes it over his head. The impact knocks Blake out of the chair and onto the floor. Blood from the head wound coats the side of his face.

Lorraine springs to her feet and rushes out of the office.

#

Half of Blake's face is covered in blood. His eyes flicker open. He pulls himself to his feet like he's crawling out of a crypt. After some effort, he gets into his chair and scans the room. Blood and shattered glass cover the already-stained carpet.

His eyes make their way around the office. He's alone.

#

Blake staggers into the bedroom and heads straight for the mirror. He takes off his shirt and examines his reflection. Using his finger, he traces the spider veins covering his chest and inch their way over his stomach. His arms and hands are also covered.

#

Now clean and dressed in a dry shirt, Blake takes his phone out of his pocket and dials a number. But as he dials the number, the phone morphs into a giant rat. Blake dials its stomach as the rat squirms in his hand.

"Get it together, man." He closes his eyes. Takes in a lung full of air. He re-opens his eyes to see the rat, still in his hand. He finishes dialing its stomach, puts the rat to his ear, and seconds later, he speaks into the rat. "Theda? This is Blake. I need you to come get me. And bring the gun I gave you."

Fifteen

Theda drives her ramshackle orange Ford Mustang. Blake is slumped in the passenger seat. He uses his hand to cover his mouth as he coughs uncontrollably. When he opens his hand, there's blood in his palm.

Theda steals a glance from the corner of her eye. "You okay?"

"No. Where's the gun?"

Theda turns her focus back onto the road. "Glove."

Blake pops open the glove compartment. Inside is a 9mm gun and an extra clip. He pulls it out and checks the ammo. It's loaded. He stuffs the extra clip in his coat pocket.

Theda says, "You wanna tell me what's at the dock?"

Blake coughs again. "The woman I love."

"You're in love? What's her name?"

"Her name's Lorraine." Blake coughs. "And I hate her."

"Sounds complicated."

Blake lays the gun in his lap and peers out the window. "It is."

#

Theda parks the car near a random assortment of boaters. She kills the engine and turns to Blake. "You look like shit."

"I've been drugged. I'm going to turn into a crazy and I don't have much time."

"Let me take you to a hospital."

Blake forces a smile. "They can't do anything. There's no cure. Yet." Theda opens her mouth to speak but Blake doesn't give her a chance. He continues. "I gotta go. Wait for me here. If I'm not back in twenty, bring the police." It takes all of his strength to open the car door and slip out.

He tries to rush through the marina with his gun drawn. Despite his efforts, he manages a little more than a shuffle. He arrives at the yacht and steps on board with his gun raised.

Five steps onto the boat and he's greeted by the sight of Miss Isaacson, Alexia, and Vic. They sit around a table and play a leisurely game of gin rummy. They don't notice Blake.

The Mermaid waves at Blake from the opposite corner of the boat.

Blake asks, "Who's winning?"

Alexia and Vic stand. Each of them reaches for their guns. Blake points his gun at them and they freeze. "Not so fast assholes."

Vic grins. "Doesn't look like you got the strength to pull the trigger."

Blake steps forward. "Wanna test your theory?" Vic loses the grin. Blake's eyes dart from Vic to Alexia to Miss Isaacson. "Where is she?"

Vic, Alexia, and Miss Isaacson exchange confused looks.

Blake says, 'My partner. Did she try to sell you the formula?"

Miss Isaacson says, "We haven't seen her since you left."

The muzzle of Blake's gun finds itself pointed at Miss Isaacson. "Are you lying to me?"

Alexia says, "She's not your partner, is she?"

"You let me worry about our dating status." Blake inches backwards.

Miss Isaacson shouts. "I want my formula! I have the money. We have an agreement. Bring me my formula!"

Blake is two feet from the dock. "You'll get your formula." The mermaid waves to him as he takes a step off the yacht. "You should be more worried about the mermaid. She has shifty eyes."

Vic, Alexia, and Miss Isaacson look around for a mermaid. There isn't one.

#

Blake shuffles across the parking lot until he's at Theda's car. With his left hand on the door handle, something catches his attention. He freezes.

Fifty feet away, a red unicorn gallops across the parking lot.

Theda says, "You getting in?"

Blake opens the door and slumps into the passenger seat.

Theda studies him. "Whatever it is, can't it wait? Let me get you some help."

"No. 5th and Dove. The building with the school bus and the crazies on the side of it."

Theda keys the ignition. "I know the one." She throws the car in drive and they peel off. "You gonna tell me what's going on?"

Blake coughs blood into his hand and examines it. Wipes it on his pants. "Remember the reporter you told me about?"

Sixteen

The rough part of town.

Newspapers dance in the wind like tumbleweeds in a dusty town. Graffiti covers parked cars, the sidewalks, and street signs. The only tree on the block has a penis drawn on it.

Theda parks the car on the side of the street. "I can get us closer to the building."

Blake has his head against the window. There's dried blood in the corners of his lips. Spider veins inch along his neck. "This is as far as you're going, Theda. I need you to turn around and go to the police station. Get Walsh. Tell him what I told you. Don't leave out any details."

"I'm not going to say anything to get you locked away."

Blake opens the door. "Tell him I made a pair of wings. Tell him I tried to touch the sun but the heat melted the glue and I fell to my death." One foot makes it out and he turns to Theda.

"Tell him I changed my name to Icarus and I'll see him in hell." He pulls the rest of his body out of the car and peers back inside. "Thanks Theda. You're the only friend I got." He slams the door shut.

A tear creeps down Theda's cheek.

Blake limps to his destination with his gun in plain sight.

#

A layer of litter covers the ground in the alley. Urban filth at its most desolate.

Blake leans against a dumpster and heaves but nothing comes out. He heaves again. This time vomit erupts out of him. He growls, dry heaves again.

In the distance, a hissing sound.

Two business professionals block the exit to the alley. They're headed his way. Both of them wear torn sports coats and tattered slacks. One brown. The other black. Blood covers both of them. Their pace is slow and awkward, but they continue to draw closer.

Once they're in range, Blake raises his gun and unloads five shots. Each bullet finds its mark. Blood turns to mist in the air as the businessmen collapse to the ground. Dead from headshots.

Blake gathers himself and steps over the bodies on his way out of the alley.

Outside of the alley, the city is post-apocalyptic. Charred automobiles line the streets. Trash is everywhere. Blood stains the sidewalks. A half-eaten liver sits against the curb.

A homeless man with a braided beard races to Blake. "I heard gunshots. Are you –" He finally notices Blake. "You look like shit."

Blake motions for him to keep his distance. "Get the police and tell them you saw a lunatic running around with a gun. Hurry. Lives are at stake."

The homeless man backpedals but never takes his gaze off of Blake.

Blake raises his gun. "Hurry, damn it. Go!"

The homeless man runs away and steals a glance over his shoulder.

Blake lumbers along until his path is blocked by two children eating the remains of a dog. They turn at the sound of his footsteps. They hiss and charge.

"Damn." Blake unloads into them until his clip is empty. They fall to the ground. Dead. He ejects the empty clip and reloads with another clip from the inside of his coat. Sounds of growls and hissing surround him. He hurries. In his weakened state, he could fall over at any moment.

The building with the school bus mural comes into view. Between Blake and the building are three women devouring scraps from an overturned trash can. A one-legged male crazy crawls towards Blake.

A quick wipe of sweat from his forehead and Blake shuffles towards the crawling crazy. It glares at him and hisses. He silences the hiss with four rounds to the face. It's dead.

But the gunshots have alerted the three trash-eating women. They turn to Blake with hungry eyes. Blake raises his gun and takes out two of them with a volley of shots. The third one charges him. He pulls the trigger.

The gun jams.

He pulls the trigger again.

Still jammed.

He tosses the gun aside and whips out his butterfly knife. He opens it as the crazy woman lunges for him. She tackles him and they fall to the ground. Blake rams the knife blade through her chin and into her mouth.

As she hisses, the blade is visible in her mouth. Using the knife to steer, Blake rolls the crazy over and climbs on top. He bashes her head into the concrete. Over and over again until her skull no longer has shape.

He sucks air into his lungs and wipes the blood from his face. A quick glance to survey the area and he pulls himself off the crazy. The gun sits only a few feet away from him.

He grabs it and checks the clip. A quick flush of the chamber to dislodge the jammed bullet and he grabs his knife. After he cleans the blood off on his sleeve, he makes his way to the building with the school bus mural on it.

A luxury car sits in front of the building. He peers through the window but finds nothing.

The children in the bus window on the mural come alive and laugh and point. Blake closes his eyes. "This

isn't happening. Keep the madness at bay until it's done."
When he re-opens his eyes, the world is back to normal.

He grimaces. Pain pulses through his right arm. It's unbearable. He lifts his right hand to take a look and his middle finger falls off. "Damn it." He grabs the finger to examine it.

It's decomposed.

He tosses it aside. Goes to the front door and attempts to open it. It's locked. He rushes to the back of the building.

In the back of the building, he finds a window. As he peers inside the building. His reflection features a version of him with spider veins covering his neck and the right side of his face.

He turns from the horrible sight. Searches the ground until he finds a rock. He tosses it through the window. Glass shatters into the building. Blake half climbs, half falls through the open window. He pulls himself to his feet and takes out his gun.

Rocks rushes into the room, revolver in hand. He positions himself so his body blocks the hallway leading out. The two men point their guns at each other.

Blake sneers. "I didn't find Arthur Preston. I came to give you a full refund."

"Cause you killed him, yeah?"

"I didn't kill him. The girl did. I only helped bury him." He takes a step towards Rocks. "You need to move out of the way."

Rocks tightens his grip on the gun. "Another step and I shoot you, yeah."

"Go ahead. I've already got a foot in the casket."

Rocks stands his ground. "You move again and your whole body will be in there."

Blake sighs. "I don't have time for this." He opens fire on Rocks. Two shots. Both hit Rocks in the chest, hurling him backwards. As he falls back, he unloads two shots into Blake, knocking him to the ground.

Both men are on the ground. Both bleed from multiple gunshot wounds.

Rocks lays motionless.

As does Blake.

Blake groans as he opens his eyes and pulls himself to a sitting position and inspects his wounds. Gunshot to the left shoulder. Another in his left rib cage. He watches Rocks. Waits for him to move.

He doesn't.

Blake coughs as he rises to his feet. He hobbles towards Rocks and points his gun at him.

Rocks coughs.

Blake pulls the trigger.

Click.

Blake pulls the trigger again.

Click.

He checks the ammo. Empty. Tosses the gun aside and takes out his butterfly knife. Rocks snickers as Blake closes in on him. He raises a pathetic hand to stop Blake, but it's no use. Blood gushes out of his mouth as Blake drives the knife into his eye socket.

A foot away is Rocks' gun. Blake grabs it and stumbles into the main section of the building.

Seventeen

Bloodied and haggard, Blake staggers into a warehouse pretending to be a laboratory.

Lorraine closes a suitcase full of cash. Next to her, Shaunassy puts the final pouch of green liquid into another briefcase. They head for the door; unaware Blake has entered the room.

Blake yells. "I lost my favorite finger because of you people."

Shaunassy and Lorraine turn around, both startled by the sight of Blake.

Lorraine feigns excitement. "Blake! You're alive!"

"Disappointed?"

Lorraine maintains the charade. "Why would you say such a thing?" She and Shaunassy backpedal towards the door.

"Because you broke a bottle over my head and left me to die."

"It was for your own good."

Shaunassy puts his hand on the doorknob.

Blake barks. "Stop right there, Shaunassy."

Shaunassy stops right there.

Blake takes a step towards them. Keeps his gun on them. "Sell people poison, drive down property values. Buy the city on the cheap, sell the cure. Hell of a business plan."

Shaunassy huffs. "Don't lecture me on the machinations of capitalism."

Blake sighs. "There's a special place in hell for people like you."

Shaunassy laughs. "When I get there, they'll serve a Fifty-year-old single malt and Sevruga Classic Grey Caviar."

"Because of you, a young woman died saving me. Her name was Cinnamon. Ring a bell?"

Shaunassy rolls his eyes. "Should it?"

Blake says, "She worked at Pettford's club. You were paying her to keep an eye on Arthur Preston, weren't you?"

Shaunassy huffs. "Why would I do such a thing? Arthur Preston worked for me. Besides, I don't deal with that layer of society." He turns to Lorraine. "What is this nonsense?"

"Don't look at her. I'm the one asking the questions."

Shaunassy steps towards Blake. "Name your price."

"I want to spend my days in heaven and my nights in hell."

With his last bit of strength, Blake pushes the crazy off of him. He tries to stand but can't. His legs give out and he topples to the ground.

The other two crazies descend upon Lorraine. She tries to push them away, but she fails. She screams as they tear her stomach open. They pull out handfuls of intestines and eat.

Blake crawls towards her, desperate to help.

A volley of gunshots fills the air. The remaining crazies are hurled backwards, away from Lorraine. Their bodies riddled with bullet holes.

Sirens wail in all directions. Cops appear. Ambulances arrive.

Walsh and Theda approach Blake. He smiles at them and uses his hand to stem the flow of blood from his neck.

Theda kneels next to him. "We're too late. I'm so sorry, Blake."

Blake forces a bloody smile. "I've been dead, Theda. Don't sweat it."

Walsh eyes the carnage. "Where's your wings?"

Blake spits out a glob of blood. "Got clipped. How is she?"

Walsh says, "Not good Blake. Not good at all."

With each inhalation, the air pushes more blood out of Blake's neck wound. The hole makes a whistling sound. "I'll take the cigarette now."

Walsh takes a pack out of his pocket, and hands a cigarette to Blake. "Didn't you quit?" He lights it for him.

"Yeah, well, something's gotta kill ya." Blake takes a long drag. Savors it. "The formula to save all the crazies is in the briefcase next to Shaunassy. You'll find him in there." He points to the building with the mural. "You have to kill me. I'm about to turn into a crazy."

Theda stands. "No Blake." She turns to Walsh. "We can get the formula."

Blake waves her off. "Don't bother. I'm full of holes and covered in bites. Put me out before –" He growls. "Before I become a rabid dog."

Detective Walsh pulls out his service pistol. Points it at Blake's head. "Sorry partner."

Blake smiles. "Don't be."

Theda turns her back. Tears in her eyes.

Walsh pulls the trigger. The bullet shatters Blake's skull. Blood and brains cover Walsh's shoes.

Cops, paramedics, and emergency service personnel clean and quarantine the area.

THE END

READ MY BOOK

One

A five-foot ceramic dolphin sits next to the fireplace. The walls, the pillows, and all of the artwork feature brightly colored flowers and botanical decor.

In the middle of the living room, Tricia has her brown hair pulled into a messy bun. A daily yoga routine has her body in tip-top shape. Her sports bra matches her floral yoga pants. She vacuums the floor like it owes her money.

Something on the floor grabs her attention. Her eyes narrow as she focuses on it. Whatever it is, she's pissed off about it. She pushes the vacuum over it. Still there. She brings the vacuum over the spot once again.

Still there.

She pauses and huffs, pushes the vacuum over it five times in rapid succession. Whatever was there, it's not there any longer.

Tricia dusts the mantle on the fireplace. When she's done, she drags her finger along the surface and inspects it for dust.

There is none.

She grins and turns her attention to the sixty-pound ceramic dolphin next to the fireplace. The duster moves over it. Her movements are quick and precise.

She rakes her finger along the dolphin's beak and inspects it for dust.

There is none.

Dolphin magnets and postcards cover the refrigerator. Dirty dishes crowd the sink and countertop.

Tricia unloads the dishwasher. Plates find their way into the cabinets. Silverware gets sorted and placed in the drawer. Before long, she's done emptying the dishwasher. Next, she loads it with dishes from the sink and counter.

Turquoise and blue are the dominant colors in the guest bedroom. A botanical pop art wallpaper covers the walls. It features various flowers in shades of blue, orange, and green. The comforter covering the queen-sized bed depicts a pair of swimming dolphins.

On the dresser are dozens of glass figurines. All of them are dolphins.

Sweat covers Tricia's face as she vacuums the floor.

Afterwards, she changes the sheets and makes the bed. The edges are crisp and the length of sheet hanging off the bed is perfectly balanced. A drill sergeant would be proud.

She takes a step back and admires her work. Something catches her eye. She leans over the side of the bed, careful not to wrinkle anything, and adjusts a wayward pillow.

The bathroom mirror gets doused with glass cleaner and wiped clean.

Now on her hands and knees, Tricia scrubs the toilet.

Hot water from the shower head soothes Tricia's face and body. She closes her eyes and sighs.

Tricia races into the kitchen with wet hair, dressed in a t-shirt and shorts. She places two salmon filets onto a baking sheet with asparagus and slides it into the oven.

The primary bedroom looks the way an aquarium would look if it only had dolphins in it. Everything is blue. Everything is dolphin-themed. It's a lot to take in.

Tricia tries on a little black dress. She stares at herself in the mirror and makes a face.

She tries on a different dress. This one has a bright seashell pattern. She's not happy with it either.

Next, she tries on a blouse with dress slacks. After a full turn in the mirror, she pokes her lip out.

Back in the mirror with another outfit change. This time she wears yoga pants and a graphic tee with a dolphin on it. She puts her hands on her hips and pushes her hip out to the side. A feeble attempt to look casual.

Instead, she achieves awkwardness.

Another wardrobe change. This time it's jeans and a tank top. She stares at herself and turns to the side. Tugs on the tank top.

Moments later, she's back in the mirror with the same pair of jeans, but now she's got on a plain white T-shirt.

Tricia races across the kitchen to the oven. She pulls out the salmon and asparagus. It's decimated. Burnt to a crisp and inedible. "Damn it. I knew I'd botch this." She closes her eyes and exhales between each word. "One. Two. Three. Four. Five." She opens her eyes and dumps the ruined dinner into the trash can.

The two-car garage only has one car in it. A mid-sized sedan that's seen better days. Moving boxes crowd the space. Tricia marches around the clutter and deposits the trash bag into the dumpster.

She scans the garage. Her eyes land on various boxes. Each one says either *mom* or *dad* on the side.

Two

A pair of stemless wine glasses sit on the countertop. Tricia fills the first with red wine. As she pours the second one, her doorbell rings.

She cheeses and straightens her shirt. "You got this." She fills the second glass with red wine and scurries out of the kitchen and across the living room.

In the foyer, she opens the front door. On the other side stands Ava. She effortlessly pulls off the casual look Tricia had made awkward. Her caramel complexion is a sharp contrast against the designer lemon yellow t-shirt. Her shoulder-length light brown hair matches her eyes. She greets Tricia with a smirk.

Tricia says, "Wow. It's you. In the flesh."

"I guess it is."

Tricia continues to stare at her for a moment. It's weird. Ava glances past her and into the living room. "So?"

This snaps Tricia back to reality. "Oh yes. Please. Sorry. Come in, come in." She steps aside.

Ava steps into the foyer and says, "You have a beautiful home. Should I take my shoes off?"

"If you don't mind."

Ava takes off her Tory Burch Eleanor sling-back leather kitten heels.

Tricia leads Ava into the living room. "Please. Make yourself at home."

Ava takes in the living room. Her eyes land on the five-foot ceramic dolphin by the fireplace. "I mean it. This place is... beautiful."

"Thanks. Sorry about the mess."

Ava scans the room. "What mess? This place is immaculate."

Shocked, Tricia brings her hand to her chest. "How sweet of you to say. I didn't have time to clean. You know how it is. With work and everything."

"Sorry. I don't even know what you do."

Tricia beams. "I'm a nurse."

"Oh. Well, thank you for your service. Do people say that to nurses?"

"Every once in a while, we hear it."

Ava can't pull her eyes away from the five-foot dolphin. "Considering what you all do, you should hear it more often."

"On the rare occasion we do hear it, it means a lot."

Tricia grabs the glasses of wine and offers one to Ava. "Wine?"

Ava accepts it with a smile. "Of course."

"It's a pinot. I hope it's okay."

"Perfect." Ava holds her glass. "What should we toast to?"

Tricia grins. "How about we toast to literature?"

Ava responds with forced warmth. "How about we toast to something more personal? Like, reconnecting."

"Sure!"

They clink glasses and take a sip. Ava takes a moment to glance around. Wherever her eyes land, there's a dolphin. Or flowers. "I like how you've decorated. It's … cheery."

Tricia takes another sip of her wine. "I can't take credit. It's my mom's doing."

"Oh."

Tricia lets her eyes wander. "She doesn't live here or anything. Neither of my parents live here. They left it to me."

"Are they no longer…"

Tricia swirls the wine around in her glass. The legs on the sides of the glass have her undivided attention. "Her and my dad, they, well. I lost them. Five years ago."

"I'm so sorry."

"It's okay. It's what they wanted."

Ava's face scrunches the way it does when she attempts to solve a puzzle. She waits for Tricia to elaborate on her odd comment.

Tricia takes another sip of her wine. The glass stays at her lips until she notices the look on Ava's face. "My mom had breast cancer. By the time they diagnosed it, it was too late. My dad didn't want to be without her. So, tailpipe. Garage. Carbon monoxide. I found them when I got home. But at least they're together. Happy endings, right?"

"I am so... I don't know what to say. I didn't mean..."

Tricia glances around the kitchen. She takes in the flowers and the dolphins. "Can we talk about something else?"

"I would love to."

"Dinner!" Tricia says, "I had this grand plan for making this amazing salmon and asparagus thing. But I got caught at work and didn't have time to cook it. Lucky for us, there's a great Chinese place with delivery. I'm buying."

"I love Chinese food," Ava says. "But you don't have to buy it."

"Please. You're giving me feedback on my manuscript. Dinner is the least I can do."

"It was only a beta read."

"I love it. Industry jargon."

Ava takes a sip of her wine. Tricia stares at her for an uncomfortable length of time.

Desperate to make it stop, Ava surveys the kitchen. Her eyes land on the dolphin-covered refrigerator. "So, dolphins, huh?"

"I'm about to have dinner with Ava Jordan."

Ava lowers her glass of wine. "Tricia. We're two old friends. I'm not anybody special. There's no reason to be nervous. Or in awe. Okay?"

"Sorry," Tricia says. "I'm being weird. I know."

"It's flattering. But it's unnecessary. You knew me long before I did… anything."

Tricia holds her phone so the screen full of Chinese restaurant Yelp reviews faces Ava. "Chinese food. Are you more of a noodle person, or a rice person?"

Ava studies the Yelp review for a local Chinese restaurant. "Definitely noodles," she says.

"Done."

#

Tricia and Ava sit on the couch, each holding a glass of wine. After a sip, Ava says, "The dances were never my thing. But you — you were it."

Tricia chuckles and waves off the comment. "Oh, please."

"Don't," Ava says. "You know how popular you were."

Tricia stares into her glass. "Those were fun times. You ever wish you could go back there?"

"To high school? Oh god no. High school was hell for me."

"Sorry." Tricia takes a nervous sip of her wine. "I forgot."

"We evolve and move on."

Tricia places her hand on Ava's leg. Leans in for emphasis. "You used that nasty rumor to create your masterpiece. Suck it, Cobb Creek Cougars."

Ava shifts. Rubs her finger over the top of her wine glass. "I don't know if I'd consider it a masterpiece. But it got solid reviews and paid off my student loans."

"You're living your dream, Ava Jordan."

Ava studies her wine glass. "Having your book turned into a movie isn't glamorous. Hollywood isn't the glitz and glam you'd imagine. Between you and me, it's a bit of a cesspool."

"Oh, come on."

"You'd be surprised."

Tricia finally pulls her hand off Ava's leg and sits back. "All the red-carpet events —" The doorbell rings. Tricia does not hide her excitement. "Chow Mein here I come."

Ava laughs.

Three

The wine is gone. On their plates are remnants of Kung Pao and drops of soy sauce. Ava leans back in her chair. Grease coats her tongue in the most satisfying way. "Thank you. This has been fun."

Tricia stands and clears the plates. "It has."

"I guess we should talk about your manuscript."

Tricia sets the dishes on the counter. "Let me get my pen and pad. Wait right there."

Tricia races out of the room.

As soon as she's gone, Ava checks the time on her phone and sighs.

Tricia returns seconds later with a pen and pad. She takes a seat across from Ava.

"Okay," Ava says. "I know this is your first book, so do you want the truth? Or do you want —"

Tricia pushes her shoulders back. "I want you to be honest with me. It's the only way I'll get better."

"You've got the right mindset," Ava says. "But please. There's two things you have to remember. One. These are only my opinions. And two. Writing is re-writing."

Tricia tilts her head back and stares at the ceiling. "Oh, my god. You hated it."

"I didn't hate it."

"I'm so embarrassed."

Ava takes out her phone and scrolls through the notepad. "I've got some suggestions to help you. Do you want to hear them?"

Tricia brings her focus back to the pen and pad. "Yes. yes. Sorry. Go ahead."

Ava pulls her attention away from the phone. "After being here with you tonight, I'm now realizing this is based on your life. At least, loosely based. Correct?"

Tricia beams with pride. "You inspired me. What's the saying? Write what you know. It's what you did."

A smile escapes Ava. "Thank you. I know for me, one of the hardest things I had to do was cut scenes and chapters I believed were vital to the story. Because I drew from my life, it all seemed important. And personal."

Tricia writes everything out of Ava's mouth. "It's too long, isn't it?"

"At six hundred pages, it's a bit much. Especially for a first-time writer. Remember. You're asking the reader to invest their time in you. And the more pages, the more expensive it is to produce."

Tricia takes notes as fast as she can. "How much should I cut out?"

"I'd say get it around three to four hundred pages."

Tricia slams her pen onto her notepad. "Oh no. What you're saying would gut my entire story."

"You have to kill your babies."

Tricia's hand goes to her chest as she searches for words. "What a horrible thing to say. Is that industry jargon?"

"It is."

Tricia grabs her pen, considers, returns it to its resting spot. Her eyes scan the room.

"Maybe you don't get it."

Ava leans back against the dolphin pillow. "Please don't say that."

Tricia leans in. "Do you? Because you haven't mentioned one thing about the characters. Or the dialogue. Because, you know. Dialogue is my strength."

Ava rolls her eyes.

Tricia doesn't notice it. "What about the dialogue? The main character, Tiffany is supposed to be witty. Wasn't she witty?"

"She had some fun moments."

"You thought she was awful."

"I wouldn't say she was awful."

Tears accumulate in the corners of Tricia's eyes. "This was a terrible idea. I should have known. I'm a no-talent hack, aren't I?"

"Tricia, I'm giving you feedback. This is what you asked for, isn't it?"

"I should stick with being a nurse. I'm an idiot for assuming I could do this." Tricia turns her attention towards the kitchen and wipes a tear from her cheek. "Who am I kidding? Writer? I need to get rid of all these crazy notions."

Ava stiffens. Rests a hand on Tricia's lap. "Your book isn't bad for a first-time writer."

"But it's obvious I'm a first-timer and a loser and I shouldn't have wasted your time with this foolish dream of mine."

Ava retrieves her glass of wine. "You can fix your story. But the first step is being open to suggestions. Nobody knocks it out of the park on a first draft."

Tricia jumps to her feet and paces the room. "No. I should be happy being a nurse. It's what I am, and it's what I'm good at. I'm not a writer. No. No. No. I'm not a writer and I'll never be good at it. I'm sorry for wasting your time with this childish dream. I haven't put in the work and it was stupid of me to presume I would be good at it because I read a bunch of books."

She stops and stares at the five-foot ceramic dolphin. "Ava, I'm sorry. I've wasted your time. I didn't even cook you dinner. I ordered Chinese takeout. Who does that? I'm the worst." She turns to Ava and forces a smile. "You should leave before I make an even bigger fool out of myself."

Ava stands. Her eyes move to the door. "Do you mind if I use the restroom really quick?"

Tricia points down the hall. "It's through there. On the right." As Ava vanishes into the darkness of the hallway, Tricia calls out, "Ava."

Ava stops. Listens.

"I'm sorry," says Tricia.

Ava vanishes into the bathroom.

When she hears the door shut, Tricia closes her eyes. "One. Two. Three. Four. Five."

#

Ava's reflection glares back at her. "Tell her what she wants to hear and get the hell out of here." She cracks her knuckles. A nervous habit she's had since she was nine.

She turns on the faucet and lets the cool water collect in her hands until it overflows.

Ava dumps the water out of her hands and turns the faucet off. "Do whatever it takes to get out of here as quickly as possible."

Four

In the kitchen, Tricia opens two pill capsules and dumps the contents into Ava's wine glass. She fills both glasses with wine and sets them on the table.

The bathroom door opens, and Ava makes her way to the kitchen. "Hey, so, I gotta go."

Tricia turns to her with a wineglass in each hand. "About what happened —"

"It's okay."

Tricia says, "It was childish. And, embarrassing."

"Sometimes these things can be tough. Especially when the project is close to your heart."

Tricia offers a glass to Ava. "I refilled your wine as a peace offering."

Ava doesn't take it. "It's unnecessary. Besides, I have to drive back."

"It would mean a lot to me if you let me get this off my chest." She takes a seat and motions for Ava to take a seat across from her.

Ava checks her phone and takes a seat.

Tricia says, "I shouldn't have acted the way I did. It was —"

"You've already apologized."

"I spend a lot of time in my head. I had this vision of how tonight was going to go, and it wasn't realistic."

"Water under the bridge."

Tricia's face lights up. "I'm happy to hear you say that." She takes a sip of her wine. With the glass at her lips, she eyes Ava.

Ava never raises the glass to her lips.

Tricia lowers the glass from her lips and says, "Is it possible to fix my story?"

"Of course."

"But I have to be open to feedback."

"Getting feedback is the hardest part of this," Ava says. "But it's also the most important. When you work with an editor, it's their job to tell you what's working and what's not. It's your job to decide what you use and what you ignore."

Tricia takes a long sip of her wine. She holds the glass at her lips and waits to see if Ava takes the bait.

She doesn't.

Finally, Tricia lowers the glass and says, "Is that what you had to do?"

"It's what every writer does."

Tricia can't take her eyes off Ava's glass. "I must seem like the worst."

Ava laughs.

Tricia takes another healthy sip of her wine.

Ava watches but never raises her glass. "Look, I know it's hard hearing your work isn't great. But if you want to do this, you have to develop thick skin."

"I should cut out some pages, huh?"

Ava says, "It would help the pacing."

Tricia shifts in her chair. Focuses on what's left in her glass. "Is this — is this something you could help me with?"

"You should enroll in my class at the college."

Tricia says, "I mean, one on one."

Ava's eyes clock the exit. "I've never taught before, so I'm going to have to see what the workload is like first."

"But if it's not too much? I know you're busy. Maybe we could meet like this once or twice a month. I'll make you dinner. No more takeout. I promise." Tricia laughs.

Ava forces herself to smile. "Let me see how the first month or two goes, we'll go from there. Fair enough?"

"I can pay you," says Tricia.

"I don't want your money, Tricia."

"You'd do it for free?"

"Depending on my schedule."

Tricia beams. She raises her glass to toast. "To reconnecting."

Ava raises her glass. They touch glasses. Tricia takes a sip.

Ava finally takes a sip. "Thanks for dinner, Tricia, but I have to get going."

"Oh, sure. Sorry to keep you. I know it's getting late. I'll walk you out."

They stand and head for the door.

Tricia leads Ava into the living room.

Ava's purse sits on the table by the couch. When she attempts to grab it, she has to steady herself.

Tricia rushes to her aid. "Are you okay?"

Ava waves her off. "Yeah. I'm fine. The blood rushed from my head or something." She raises her purse and promptly drops it. As she goes to grab it again, she collapses onto the couch.

Tricia takes a seat next to her. "Wait right here. I'll get you some water."

Ava tries to grab Tricia's arm, but she doesn't have the strength. Instead, she passes out on the couch.

Five

Ava lies on top of the bed in the guest bedroom. Her body covers the comforter with the pair of swimming dolphins. She's passed out with her right leg shackled to the bed frame.

Finally, she stirs. Her eyes open and she notices the shackles. "What the fuck?"

Panic as she pulls on the chain connecting her to the bed. After five tugs, she drops the chain and notices Tricia, in a chair on the opposite side of the room. Eyes glued on Ava.

Ava scowls at her. "What's going on? Did you drug me?"

"Must have been the Chinese food."

"It wasn't the damn Chinese food."

Tricia grins at Ava. "In your book, the Vanessa character is me, isn't it?"

Ava falls back into the bed and stares at the ceiling. "Is that what this is about?"

"Be honest. It's me."

Ava keeps her eyes on the ceiling. "It is you. What happens now?"

"The character was a total bitch, but I get it. You gotta embellish some things to keep the pages turning. I knew it was me. When the movie came out, people I don't even remember from high school were getting in touch. I was getting calls and emails for six months."

Ava finally meets Tricia's gaze. "What's this? Your elaborate revenge plot?"

Shock covers Tricia's face. "Revenge? Oh god no. You putting me in your book was the best thing that ever happened to me. Until now."

"Now?"

Tricia says, "You volunteered to help me with my book."

"Volunteered? You chained me to the bed."

Tricia stands. "We have work to do and I need you to focus." She makes her way to the door. "Get some rest, Ava. We're going to get started bright and early."

Tricia opens the door and heads out.

Ava yells after her. "Where's my purse?"

Tricia slams the door shut behind her.

"Tricia!"

No answer.

"This isn't funny. Come back here."

Silence.

"I'm serious. You can't do this. Come back." Ava waits for a response. It never comes. "Tricia! Get in here!"

She waits.

"Tricia! You'll never get away with this! People will wonder where I am! Tricia!" Frantic, Ava tries to free herself. First, she tries to pull her leg through the shackle, but it's too tight.

She gets onto the floor and tests the length of slack. Her first move is to make it to the door, but the amount of slack only allows her to get halfway around the room. Dejected, she takes a seat on the floor next to the bed and examines the bed and the shackles.

Even if she could lift the bed, it wouldn't matter. She pulls the chain again. "You don't have to do this! I'll help you with your book!"

No answer.

She tries to lift the bed but only gets it about an inch and a half off the ground before she drops it.

#

Tricia kneels beside her bed. Eyes closed. Hands clasped in prayer. "Mom, Dad, things are coming together for me. My friend Ava, the famous writer, agreed to help me with my story. It's going to be amazing. And I'm going to sell it. I'll prove to you I can get out of this town. And not only will I survive in the big city, I'll flourish. Watch. You'll see."

Six

The digital clock on the nightstand reads 4:58 AM.

Tricia stares at it for a moment before rolling over. Her eyes focus on the dolphin wallpaper.

After a moment, she rolls back over to face the clock.

4:59 AM.

Her eyes plead with time to move faster. Seconds pass at a snail's pace.

5:00 AM.

The traffic report shoots out of the clock radio speakers. There's an overturned semi-truck. Tricia rises to an upright position and shuts it off.

In the primary bathroom, Tricia scrubs her teeth with vigor. Blood and toothpaste seep out of her mouth and into the sink.

Tricia performs the lotus position on her yoga mat in the middle of the living room floor. Inhale through the nose. Exhale through the mouth.

The scent of bread perfectly evolved into toast wafts through the kitchen. At the table, Tricia takes a bite out of her egg sandwich with mustard greens and avocado. She savors each bite and chases it with orange juice.

Tricia stands at the door to the guest bedroom. She holds a tray with another egg sandwich and a glass of orange juice. Hand on the doorknob.

She opens the door and marches into the bedroom.

Ava sits with her back to the headboard and arms folded. She stares at Tricia.

Tricia says, "Look at you. Ready to welcome the day."

"I couldn't sleep."

"Me either. Isn't this exciting?" Tricia stands at the foot of the bed. Grins from ear to ear. "I brought you some breakfast. It'll help with the hangover."

"I'm not hungover."

Tricia says, "It's an egg sandwich with mustard greens and avocado." She sets the tray next to Ava and takes a seat.

Ava scowls at the food. "I'm not eating this."

"The avocado," Tricia says, "contributes to healthy blood flow to the brain. It also helps lower blood pressure."

"I don't trust you," Ava says.

"We've got a lot of work to do. It's important your brain is firing on all cylinders."

Ava pushes the tray away from her. "Have you heard anything I've said?"

Tricia scoots the tray back towards Ava. "Don't be a martyr. I know you're hungry."

"Tricia, you need to let me go."

"Fine." Tricia snatches the sandwich and takes a bite. With each bite, her mouth opens wide enough to see the mush inside. It's the most dramatic chewing ever.

Ava watches with disgust.

For an encore, Tricia performs an equally dramatic swallow, opens her mouth, and sticks out her tongue so Ava can see it's gone. "Happy?"

"How do you imagine this working?"

Tricia pats Ava on the leg. "You're gonna help me improve my manuscript. Once it's in a good place, you can leave." Tricia stands and smoothes out her vacated spot on the bed. "I'll let you enjoy your breakfast. When I return, be ready to help me create a masterpiece!"

Ava glances at the food and back at Tricia.

Tricia says, "Thank you for doing this. It means the world to me." She turns and marches out.

When the door closes, Ava turns her attention to the sandwich. She examines the bite Tricia took out of it. After a moment, she takes off the top part of the sandwich and removes the egg and the mustard greens.

A dissected version of the sandwich sits on her plate. She pushes the food around with her finger.

The door opens. Ava flinches.

Tricia stands in the doorway. Bucket in one hand. Roll of toilet paper in the other. "I'm afraid the chain won't reach the little girl's room, so..." She pats the side of the bucket and sets it next to the bed. "Don't worry. It's no different from cleaning out a bedpan. I'll take it out a couple times a day so you don't have to worry about the smell."

Ava says, "Have you lost your mind?"

"Treat it like a writer's retreat. Like Mary Shelley and those guys." Tricia marvels at the room as if it's her first time here. "My house will be our own little Villa Diodati." Her eyes land on the sandwich. "You prefer your sandwiches deconstructed. Noted. Okay. I'll leave you to it. Eat. I'll be back in…" She checks her watch. "Thirty-seven minutes." She scampers out of the room.

Ava reassembles her deconstructed sandwich and takes a healthy bite.

Seven

Ava paces. As much as the chain will allow.

The door opens and Tricia struts in. Pen and pad in hand. She smirks at the sight of Ava. "Exercise is good. Gets the blood flowing. Studies have shown exercise is vital for those who embark on creative endeavors."

"Fuck off."

The tray and empty plate are on the bed. Tricia says, "I see you ate your breakfast. Good. Can't have you hangry." Her cackle fills the room. "We would get nothing done." She takes a seat on the edge of the bed. Rests the pad in her lap.

Ava stands across from her.

Tricia says, "You prefer to stand?"

"I'm not helping you."

"You volunteered."

Ava says, "To help you when I had time. Not be your prisoner."

Tricia opens the pad and readies her pen. "I'm not asking for much of a commitment from you."

"You're gonna get me fired before my first official day. I have meetings to get to."

Tricia sighs. "Meetings? Classes don't start for another eight days. It's plenty of time."

"I'm a new professor. I have meetings with my department head. There's a new professor orientation."

Tricia keeps her attention focused on the notepad. "Guess you'll have to miss those."

Ava leans onto the bed so her eyes meet Tricia's. "This is my life you're messing with."

"Ava, what we do here is bigger than some job at a junior college."

"This is your story. Not mine."

Tricia closes the notepad and sets her pen on top of it. "I see what's going on here. How about this? We co-write it. I should have offered this to you before. I apologize. I'm still learning the industry etiquette."

Ava straightens and covers her face with her hands. "I don't want to co-write your shitty novel."

"It's why you're here. To turn my shitty novel into a masterpiece."

"I'm here because you drugged me."

Tricia points the notepad at Ava. "You're here because you volunteered."

Ava barks, "Stop saying that."

Tricia stands. "I can see you're agitated. Nothing creative can come from an environment like this. I'm going to leave. Give you time to process what's going on. It's a lot. I want you to know I understand where you're coming from. I'll come back in an hour or two and we'll get to work. But before I leave, I want you to think about something."

"Oh yeah?"

Tricia arrives at the door and turns. "The sooner we finish, the sooner you can leave. Classes are in eight days. I'd hate for you to get fired before you even start. Can you imagine the headlines? Flash in the pan writer can't even keep a job at a junior college. I would never say such a thing about you, but you know how these sites are. With the clickbait and the hashtags." She lets herself out.

Eight

Tricia sits at the kitchen table. Her fingers type at warp speed. Eyes narrow as her focus intensifies.

The right hand comes off the keyboard, and her index finger finds its way into her mouth. She gnaws on the nail until it bleeds. "Shit."

She examines the wound. A drop of blood lands on her keyboard. A swipe of the finger and it's gone.

Tricia takes a moment to read what's on the screen. Midway through, her eyes shut. Her teeth grind. She jumps out of her chair and paces the kitchen. Her eyes never leave the laptop screen.

#

Ava lies on the bed in the guestroom with her head buried in the pillow.

The sound of Tricia's voice fills the room. "This is why you never left. Why you're still stuck in this dead-end town? You don't deserve better. You haven't put in the work. Stop kidding yourself. You suck at this, Tricia. You suck at life. You should die."

Ava strains to listen as Tricia continues.

"Stupid. Stupid. Stupid."

Silence.

Ava stares at the door.

Footsteps make their way towards the door. The doorknob turns and in steps Tricia. Pen and notepad in hand. "Are we doing better?"

Ava studies her. "Are you?"

"I'm wonderful. Ready to crack this story."

"What were those things you were saying?"

"It appears the biggest issue with my story is the way it opens." Tricia takes a seat at the end of the bed.

Ava pushes herself back against the headboard. "What I heard didn't sound healthy. Are you seeing somebody about what you're experiencing?"

Tricia laughs. "It's part of my process. Now. About the beginning."

"If you need someone to talk to."

"I want to talk about my novel. For fuck's sake." Tricia shakes out her hands. "The beginning of my story. I need your help."

Ava pulls her knees into her chest. "Okay. Act one."

"The beginning," Tricia says, "Is the source of all the issues in the story."

"I wouldn't disagree."

Tricia scribbles it into her notes. "Great. We've diagnosed the problem."

"One of the problems."

Tricia keeps her eyes on the notebook. "No need to be hateful." She finally looks from her notepad. "How do I fix it? Tell me. I want to learn."

"Are you familiar with the story circle?"

Tricia says, "Never heard of it."

"How about the hero's journey?"

"I've heard of it, but I'm not intimately familiar with it."

Ava relaxes and lets her legs stretch out. "We'll start with the basic three-act structure."

Tricia scribbles it onto the page. "Keep going."

"It breaks your story into four sections. The first section is your first act, there's the first half of your second act. There's the second half of the second act. It comes right after the midpoint. Last, you have the third act or the climax.

Tricia glances at Ava. "Did your story use this?"

"Every story uses it. Or at least, some version of it."

"Got it."

Ava gives Tricia time to get it on paper. "Now. Your first act needs to serve multiple functions. We have to establish your protagonist's normal life. We have to establish the theme. We need to show what the character wants. There has to be an inciting incident. And before the character goes on their journey, they have to first debate whether to go at all."

Tricia uses her fingers to massage her temples. "All of this is in the first act?"

"It is."

"I didn't do any of those things."

Ava emits a cackle. "You didn't. It's why your story doesn't work. Your main character doesn't have a want or need."

"She wants to become a doctor."

Ava turns her body and sits upright so her legs can hang off the edge of the bed. "Her drive to become a doctor isn't clear until the third act. What you have is a passive protagonist." She stands and stretches her back. "Your main character floats through life. Things happen to her until out of nowhere she decides, oh, I want to become a doctor."

Tricia stiffens. "She has to overcome hardships."

"Those hardships have to be obstacles she must overcome to achieve her goal."

Tricia stands. Rubs her face with her hands. "She's a survivor."

"The way it's written now, she peaked in high school." Ava lays back on the bed with a smirk.

Tricia says, "She did not peak in high school."

Ava stares at the ceiling. "The scenes and sequences after she graduates are the same note. Over and over again. She's weak."

Tricia paces. "She's not weak."

"Oh yeah? Have you ever counted how many times she cries in this thing?"

Tricia whirls around and says, "It's important to show how these things affect her. Look at what happens to her. And she still makes something of herself."

Ava meets Tricia's eyes. "She doesn't make any decisions. She has no goals. No ambitions. And the reason all these things happen to her is because she never tries to fix her situation. She has the means to leave the town, but she never does. It's what makes her weak."

Tricia grits her teeth. "It's a story about a woman who overcomes hardships to become someone greater. She wants to be a doctor. It's in the book."

"If this is what the story needs, the decision to become a doctor needs to happen much earlier," says Ava.

"This would change my entire story."

"You asked for my help. You got it."

Tricia surrenders to the edge of the bed. "And this will improve my story?"

"Exponentially."

Tricia slaps her hands on her thighs. "I'll do it."

"Great. I'd like some privacy. I have to use the bucket."

Nine

Tricia sits on the floor of the living room. She faces the giant ceramic dolphin and whispers, "She says this will help my story. But, I gotta say, it doesn't sound like my story anymore."

Tricia sighs and lies on the floor. She stretches her arms back as far as they'll go. "I need to write this novel and get out of this town. I'm gonna prove all of you wrong."

She pulls herself to her feet and trudges into the kitchen, where her laptop waits. Open and ready.

After she plops into the chair, she locks her fingers, pushes them out, and listens to them all crack. "Take the advice. She's a pro. You're a nurse who knows nothing."

#

The acrid scent of feces and urine pollutes the air.

Ava lies on the floor by the wall. She strips away shards of wallpaper. There's a knock at the door. She doesn't even flinch. "What?"

"Are you finished with the bucket? I want to take it out for you."

Ava tears off a quarter-inch chunk of wallpaper. "All yours."

The door opens and Tricia steps inside. The damage to her wallpaper puts her on edge. "What are you doing?"

"I'm bored."

"It's rude to destroy someone's belongings."

Ava tears away another strip of wallpaper.

Tricia races towards her. "Stop it!"

Ava stops and rolls over. She stares at the ceiling. "Can I get my phone?"

"I don't have any more of this wallpaper. I'm going to have to redo the entire wall."

Ava says, "Art is about sacrifice."

Tricia says, "This is so disrespectful. Why would you peel it?"

"You chained me to a bed." Ava pulls herself onto the bed. She makes sure her chains rattle for emphasis.

"Art is about sacrifice," Tricia smirks.

Ava seethes. "Could you bring me some magazines? A book? Something?"

Tricia shifts her focus from Ava to the bucket. "I would prefer you be one hundred percent focused on my story. It'll help you get out of here faster."

"What am I supposed to do when you're working on the new pages?"

Ava doesn't move her feet as Tricia tries to sit on the bed. She's forced to make room for Ava's feet, so her butt lands half-way off the mattress.

Tricia tries to balance on the edge of the bed. "I suppose I could print some crossword puzzles. What do you say?"

Ava finally moves her legs. "Anything is better than staring at the ceiling."

"Are you hungry?"

"Starving."

Tricia smiles. "There's some leftover Chinese food. Would you like some?"

"Sure. Whatever."

Tricia leaps to her feet and bows. "My pleasure, milady."

#

Water pools in Tricia's eyes as she reheats the Chinese food in the skillet.

The crossword puzzles sit on the nightstand in the guest bedroom.

Ava devours her food. She only stops when she notices Tricia's food remains untouched. Ava goes back to shoveling noodles into her mouth.

Tricia sighs.

Forkful after forkful of noodles vanish into Ava's mouth.

Tricia sighs even louder.

Ava ignores it and slurps Chow Mein into her mouth.

Tricia sighs a third time. This time even more dramatically than the previous two.

With a mouth full of noodles, Ava asks, "You okay?"

Tricia turns to her. Eyes puffy from crying. "It's my story."

"Of course it is."

Tricia buries her head in her hands. "This is no time to make jokes. I'm watching my dream evaporate before my eyes."

"Now you're being dramatic."

Tricia attempts to regain her composure. She fails. "At first I was going to tell my story as a screenplay. But a few days later, May 27th rolled around."

"The anniversary of your parents' death?"

Confusion covers Tricia's face. "No. Our graduation day."

Ava laughs until Tricia's confusion makes her stop. "Oh."

They stare at each other.

Tricia can't believe Ava doesn't remember it.

Ava can't believe Tricia remembers it.

It's awkward.

Finally, Tricia says, "So I'm watching your movie and in my head it's all like, you know, if Ava Jordan can write a book..." She pushes the noodles around on her plate.

Ava does not hide how insulted she is.

Tricia continues, "I'm realizing my life wouldn't make a great book."

Ava loads another forkful of noodles. "Most people's lives wouldn't even make a mediocre book."

"I thought I was different."

"You're not."

Tricia stands. "If I'm not going to write my book, there's no reason to keep you here."

With the fork in her mouth, Ava says, "You're letting me go?"

Tricia fills her lungs with air. "I'm going to sleep on it. In the morning, if I still feel the same way, you'll be free to leave."

Ava eyes her. "What are the chances of this? Percentage-wise."

"I'm too depressed to do math." Tricia motions towards her plate of Chinese food. "In case you need a midnight snack."

Ava shovels the food onto her plate.

#

Tricia lays in bed face down on top of the sheets, still dressed as she was earlier.

She chuckles and rolls over. The chuckle morphs into maniacal glee.

Ten

It's the middle of the night and Ava is fast asleep. She rolls over and hits something. Her eyes open to see Tricia in bed next to her with a huge grin on her face. Their noses are only inches apart as Tricia stares at her.

Ava freaks out. Pushes Tricia away and says, "What the fuck are you doing?"

Tricia's eyes are wild, and her grin widens. "I've been going about this all wrong."

Tricia's demeanor puts Ava on edge. "This couldn't wait until —"

"I don't want your help with my story."

Ava relaxes. "You're letting me go?"

"At first, I wanted your help. But now I realize you need this as much as I do."

Disappointment washes over Ava. "Tricia —"

Tricia leans in and whispers, "We should be writing a novel together."

Ava stares at her in disbelief.

Tricia says, "I knew you'd be on board."

"I'm not on board with this. I want to go home."

"You can go home," Tricia pulls her body to a sitting position and puts her hand on Ava's shoulder. "Right after we finish the first draft."

Fury wells inside of Ava. She smacks Tricia's hand off her shoulder. "No. I'm not doing this. A first draft could take months."

"We'll knock it out much quicker. You and me. Working together. Three days tops. You haven't seen me type. I'm fast. Like, secretary in the fifties fast."

Ava says, "If you want it to be good —"

"It's only the first draft. When we're done, you can go. We'll need a new set of eyes for feedback. Once you're gone, you and I can handle the rest through email." Tricia's body rocks back and forth. She can hardly contain herself.

"I'm going to lose my job because of you."

Tricia grabs both of Ava's hands and pulls them towards her. "This will be your big comeback. And, it'll be my introduction to the literary world. Two birds. One stone."

Ava yanks her hands-free. "Do you have any idea how long it takes to decide what to write?"

"There's two of us. It should cut the time in half."

Ava says, "It doesn't work that way."

"All we need," Tricia says, "is a quick brainstorming session. It'll be easy. Look how inspired we are."

Ava falls back into the bed. "I'm not inspired. I'm exhausted."

"I've got the perfect remedy."

#

Tricia uses a coffee grinder to pulverize fresh coffee beans. Under the hum of the grinder, she says, "I deserve abundance. I deserve success. I deserve happiness. I deserve abundance. I deserve success. I deserve happiness. I deserve abundance. I deserve success. I deserve happiness."

Eleven

A corkboard sits against the wall. Notecards cover the bed.

Ava takes a sip of her coffee.

Tricia paces. Her energy is manic. "We should do something creepy. A thriller. Something Alfred Hitchcock would make. Oooh. Like Strangers on a Train. I'm gonna write this down."

She scribbles it onto a notecard and posts it on the corkboard.

The corkboard now features a notecard with the words: *STRANGERS ON A TRAIN*

Tricia paces the room some more. "But I'd like for it to have a romantic element. Oh. What if we did a romantic comedy? I should write this down."

Seconds later, the corkboard has a notecard with the words: *ROMANTIC COMEDY*

Tricia paces some more. "If we go the romantic comedy route, it puts a lot of pressure on us to be funny. And you seem to lean more towards dark dramatic material. Do you think you could handle lighter, more fun material?"

Ava responds with a prolonged sip of her coffee.

Tricia says, "Yeah. Me neither." She takes the *Romantic Comedy* card off of the board. "Maybe we should go the antihero route? You know, someone readers will love even though they're being crazy. Or evil. How fun!"

Ava stares into her coffee mug.

Tricia writes on a notecard. "An...ti...he...ro." She takes the notecard and pins it onto the corkboard.

Ava glances up from her mug. "Why don't we write about a no-talent hack who kidnaps an author and forces her to collaborate on a novel?" She takes another sip of her coffee.

Tricia stares at Ava.

Ava replies with a smirk and takes another sip of her coffee.

Tricia says, "We can draw from our own experiences! People always say, write what you know." Tricia marvels at Ava's genius. "You are so brilliant. You deserve everything coming to you."

"Thanks."

Tricia shakes the excitement out of her hands. "Can it be from my character's point of view?"

"Sure."

Tricia holds out her hand. "Deal." They shake. Tricia grins as the shake continues for an abnormal amount of time. "What are our next steps?"

"First, you let go of my hand."

"Oh. Sorry. I'm just... ugh. This is incredible. This journey we're about to embark on will be life-changing. And life-affirming. All the life things."

Ava says, "Sure. But first, we need to organize our scenes into a beat sheet or outline."

Tricia raises her notecards. "Let's do this. First scene, my character — let's call her Tina."

"Subtle."

"It's a placeholder," Tricia says. "My character gets ready for the writer to come over. She's vacuuming, and cleaning, and whatnot."

"Weren't you at work all day and didn't have time to clean?"

Tricia breaks eye contact with Ava and turns her attention to her notecards. "Oh. Yeah. Well, we want to show how important this meeting is. Nothing wrong with a little embellishment."

"Whatever you need to tell yourself."

"Now. Our main character, Tina, prepares for her friend from college," She winks at Ava. "to come over. I figure we could change a few of the finer details, so it's not so on the nose."

"Fine," says Ava.

"And this is when your character arrives. What should we call her?"

"What about Eve?"

Tricia's jaw falls open. "I love it. Gives the whole thing a biblical subtext. Wow! You truly are great."

Ava sips her coffee.

#

Notecards cover the corkboard. Tricia stands next to it and admires her work.

Ava lays across the bed, bored out of her mind. "We're at the point where Eve goes to the bathroom, right?"

"We are."

"And while she's in the bathroom," Ava says, "is when Tina slips something into her drink."

"Tina is not the type who would poison someone."

Ava says, "She's definitely the type to poison someone."

"I disagree."

"She's pretty desperate," says Ava.

Tricia folds her arms. "She is not desperate."

"She's extremely desperate."

Tricia stiffens. "I would categorize her as more... determined."

"More like... desperate, with a hint of determination."

Tricia says, "She knows what she wants. We shouldn't fault her for being passionate."

"We should fault her because Eve finds herself chained to the bed."

Tricia balls her hand into a fist. Unaware she's crushing a notecard. "For her own good. Besides, Tina couldn't have poisoned her. She's a surgeon, and surgeons take oaths."

Ava says, "An oath she broke. Who else chained Eve to the bed?" She rattles her chains.

"Maybe the pizza Eve and Tina ate was a little... off." Tricia attempts to reopen the notecard.

"And yet, Tina has no symptoms." Ava takes another sip of her coffee.

"That Eve knows of."

Ava says, "But this doesn't explain why Eve is chained to the bed. Could be a major plot hole if we don't write from a place of honesty."

Tricia admits defeat on the notecard. She folds it and slips it into her back pocket. "Perhaps Tina saw an opportunity. After all, she is determined."

"This makes her the villain in our story."

Tricia stomps her foot. "Not if it's an opportunity to change both their lives. For the better, I might add. Maybe Eve should thank Tina for going to such lengths. After all, Eve returned home with her tail between her legs."

Ava grits her teeth. "I need to use the bucket."

Tricia trudges to the door and forces a demonic smile. "I'll make some breakfast."

"I'd also like to take a shower."

Tricia freezes. With her hand on the doorknob, she keeps her back to Ava. "But we're on such a roll."

"I can smell myself."

"I'm not stupid. You're going to try and escape."

Ava says, "I can't be at my best if I don't feel like I'm at my best."

Tricia turns to her. "Not until we finish the outline."

"You promise?"

"I promise. Now. How about another sandwich?"

Twelve

Tricia cuts an avocado and scoops it onto a plate. She sets it between mustard greens and a sunny-side-up egg. With care and precision, she fans the avocadoes out so they resemble a flower. "I am not a bad person. I'm determined. I'm driven. I'm smart. And I'm likable. I am not a bad person. I'm determined. I'm driven. I'm smart. And I'm likable."

She places two pieces of toast on the plate.

#

Ava eats the last of her deconstructed sandwich.

Tricia sits at the end of the bed. "This is wild. We're writing a story about us writing the story, about us writing the story."

With a mouth full of mustard greens, Ava says, "And it's every bit as stupid as it sounds."

"It could be the greatest thing ever made."

"Or the worst."

Tricia says, "It's what makes this so inspired."

"If you say so."

Tricia refers to her notebook. "And you're saying the midpoint needs to be a dramatic shift in the story?"

"If it's a tragic ending, the midpoint should give us a false sense that it's all going to be okay. If it's an uplifting ending, the midpoint should be the opposite."

Tricia glances from her notes. "But we don't know the ending."

"For now, the midpoint should be the decision to do away with the original manuscript, and for Tina and Eve to write a new story together."

Tricia scribbles this in her notes. "This means the next scene after the midpoint is them coming up with ideas for the new book."

"They decide to write a novel about them writing a novel."

Tricia writes as fast as she can. "Next, the outline."

"And Eve asks for a shower but gets denied."

"She doesn't get denied. They make a deal."

Ava says, "Tina refuses to let Eve have a shred of humanity."

Tricia rolls her eyes. "They agree to do it after the outline. Wait. This would be the next scene. This. Very. Moment."

Ava swallows the last of her deconstructed sandwich. "I guess it is."

"What do we do now?"

"We've outlined all we can outline. Which means I'm owed a shower."

Tricia sets her notebook on the bed. Studies the corkboard on the other side of the room. "The outline isn't done."

"You have enough to write," Ava says. "We'll get more scenes as things happen. This entire thing will have to be fluid."

"You're right. For something this original, the old rules don't apply."

Ava tugs at her shackles. "Great. Now let me out of these shackles so I can take a shower."

"I promised I'd let you get clean."

#

In the primary bathroom, Tricia fills a bucket with water in the bathtub. "This isn't stupid. It's inspired. She's jealous because she didn't come up with this great idea. She's frustrated with how her life has turned out and she's taking it out on you. But it's okay. You're going to save her. And you'll become best friends."

A black trash bag gets cut along the edge until it opens enough to resemble a large black tarp. Tricia lays it on the floor in the guest bedroom.

Cut open black trash bags cover half of the floor. The bucket of water occupies a spot on the floor next to the bed. A bar of soap sits on the bed.

Tricia grabs a sponge off the bed. She offers it to Ava.

"What happened to the shower?" Ava says.

"This is the best I can do. Take it or leave it."

Ava eyes the sponge. "You're not giving me a sponge bath."

"You're right, I'm not." Tricia thrusts the sponge at Ava. "You're gonna give yourself a sponge bath. Take it."

Ava accepts the sponge.

Tricia takes a seat on the opposite end of the bed, away from the designated sponge bath area.

Ava pulls her shirt over her head. She stops before she gets to her jeans. "I'm not doing this in front of you."

Tricia laughs. "Oh, come off it, Ava. I'm a nurse. This isn't the first time I've seen a naked woman."

"Get out."

"It's not a big deal," Tricia says. "Besides, our story could use a little sexual tension." She laughs.

Ava doesn't.

Tricia says, "The sooner we get done with the manu-script, the sooner you can leave. And we have a lot of work to do." She turns and faces the opposite direction so her back is to Ava. "Better?"

Ava glares at Tricia as she unbuttons her jeans and slides them to the bottom of the chain. She removes her bra and panties. Her panties won't come all the way off either. She leaves them around the chain above the jeans. Her eyes stay trained on Tricia. "You're not a nurse, are you?"

"What a rude thing to say."

Now nude, Ava says, "You haven't left for work since I got here."

Tricia continues to face the opposite direction. "I'm using my vacation days. How long should the book be?"

Ava dips the sponge into the bucket of water. "Did you plan to do this to me, or was it an impulse decision after you heard my feedback?"

Tricia's hands grip the sheet as she makes a fist. "There was no plan. Things sort of happened. Can we move on now?"

Ava uses the sponge to clean herself. "And you randomly have shackles lying around?"

"How long should the book be?"

Ava says, "Why are you trying to change the subject?"

"I'm not. I'm working on our novel. As you should be."

Ava says, "A book like this should be about two-hundred pages."

Tricia slumps her shoulders. "Seems too short. I'd like for it to be at least three-hundred. Maybe even four-hundred."

Ava glances from her toilet bucket to her water bucket. She squeezes the sponge so the water drips into the toilet bucket. She dips the sponge into the water bucket. "Where'd you get the shackles?"

"I bought them. Years ago."

Ava scrubs her legs. "I'm not the first person you've done this to?"

"Some would say I take the annual Halloween Fair a bit too seriously."

Ava scrubs her other leg, but her eyes drill holes into the back of Tricia's head. "This concept can't sustain such a long book. Most of it's going to be two people talking in one room. We should make it a novella. Or a short story. Get in and get out."

Tricia says, "The shorter it is, the faster you can leave."

"True, but I'm not wrong about the page length."

Tricia sighs. "I hope such brevity still allows us to dive into the complexities of the characters."

Ava squeezes the sponge out into the bathroom bucket. "We'll be fine. They're not that complex."

"We'll have to agree to disagree. The inciting incident. Is it when Eve wakes up chained to the bed?"

Ava grabs the towel off the bed and dries herself. "We can use it if we need to. But a better-inciting incident is when Tina loses her shit after getting feedback."

"She doesn't lose her shit."

Ava laughs. "What would you call it?"

Tricia turns to face Ava. Fury in her eyes. "She's passionate about her work."

"Fine. The inciting incident," Ava says. "is when Tina's passion overflows and shows she's unstable."

"Are you trying to get a rise out of me?"

Ava says, "I'm trying to finish this manuscript so I can get the hell out of here. It's important we show what the antagonist is capable of."

Tricia says, "The antagonist? You mean the villain?"

"Every story needs one."

"And you're saying it's Tina?"

Ava says, "The story only has two people." She tosses the wet towel onto the floor. "And it's certainly not the one who wakes up chained to the bed." She pulls her panties up the chain and puts them on.

"Fine. The most interesting characters are the bad guys, anyway." Tricia watches Ava as she puts her bra on. "Your skin is flawless."

"Weren't you facing the other way?"

"Are you not done?"

Ava fastens her bra. "You've got enough to write the first act."

"You sure?"

"Yes."

Tricia hustles over to the corkboard. "Mind if I take this?"

"Have at it, kiddo."

Thirteen

Tricia pounds away at the keyboard. She is inspired. Focused. Driven.

Her archaic printer spits out page after page. Tricia beams as each page rolls off the assembly line.

#

Ava stares straight ahead. "I'm not reading it."

Across the bedroom stands Tricia. Manuscript in hand. "I'm doing all the writing. The least you can do is give it a read and give me some feedback."

"Only if you do something for me first."

Tricia says, "This is a partnership."

"This is a hostage situation."

"Now who's being dramatic?"

"I'm not reading those pages," Ava says, "unless you give me my phone."

Tricia laughs. "I'm not giving you your phone."

"I'm not reading the pages."

Tricia tosses the manuscript onto the bed. "This is our work. Our blood, sweat, and tears. Don't you want to make sure it meets your standards before you put your name on it?"

Ava holds out her hand. Palm raised. "Phone."

"You're gonna call for help. I'm not stupid."

"I've had no contact with the outside world. I could lose my job," Ava says. "People could be looking for me."

Tricia says, "I watch the 11 o'clock news. Trust me. Nobody is looking for you."

"You don't watch the news at night."

Tricia laughs. "You don't know what I do when I leave this room."

"Let me check my emails."

"No."

Ava pulls herself to the edge of the bed. She gazes at the floor and says, "You can sit next to me. I don't care. Read the emails before I send them to make sure I'm not asking for help. It doesn't matter to me. I can't lose this job."

Tricia softens. "I'm going to sit next to you and read them as you type."

"You'll be bored to tears, but it's fine with me."

#

Ava's phone is plugged into the wall by the bed. She scrolls through it.

Tricia sits next to her. Eyes fixated on the screen. "I know how you see me, and it's not what I am. I'm a nice person."

"A nice person who drugged me and chained me to a bed."

"You wouldn't have helped me."

Ava stops scrolling to type an email. "You don't know that."

"In your eyes, I'm a no-talent hack."

The email has Ava's full attention. "You have a lot to learn. And you can't handle feedback. But the real issue is, you have a lot of stuff to work out."

Tricia rubs her temples. "I know. The first act isn't where it needs to be."

"I'm not talking about story structure."

"Oh."

Ava finally shifts her gaze away from the phone and onto Tricia. "You need to see somebody."

"I'm fine."

"You're not fine."

"You're a famous author and screenwriter. You have no concept of what real people go through."

Ava turns her attention back to her phone. "And you have no idea what high school was like for me, do you?"

Tricia puts her hand on Ava's leg. "I know what people said about you. I know... kids can be ruthless."

"Ruthless is an understatement."

Tricia squeezes Ava's leg. "I'm sorry you went through such a tough time. But you did profit from it. You wrote a book based on your experiences. They even hired you to write your own movie."

Ava wards off the tears as she forces a chuckle. "Yeah. I was on top of the world for a year or so. But you want to know what happened afterwards? I couldn't even sell a pitch. I wrote five spec scripts. Nothing. A handful of rewrite assignments. I still haven't had another book idea. Now look at me. Barely holding on to a teaching job at a junior college."

"Teaching is admirable work."

Ava brushes a tear off her cheek. "You know why I came back here?"

"Because you're a good person and you want to help the community."

Ava howls. "Yeah right. I still get checks from my one book and the movie. It's enough to buy the biggest house in the zip code. Drive the nicest car. Wear the nicest clothes. I'm here because I want the people here to know this shit hole town didn't destroy me." She sneers at Tricia. "Hollywood may have chewed me up and spit me out, but not this place. I want these townies to see that when they pass me in the grocery store."

"Like it or not, this town made you who you are."

"I'm sending this email."

Tricia says, "It passed inspection."

Ava hits send and hands the phone back to Tricia.

Tricia drops the manuscript into Ava's lap. "Don't let your bitterness blind you to the fact we're doing something special."

Fourteen

Tricia does the mountain pose on her mat in the middle of the living room floor. Inhale through the nose. Exhale through the mouth.

She extends her leg and moves into Warrior One. Her hands connect over her head. Her eyes shut. Inhale through the nose. Exhale through the mouth.

Tricia moves her hips to the side of the mat and positions herself in Warrior Two. She extends her arms out to her sides. Inhale through the nose. Exhale through the mouth.

#

Ava lies on the bed, flat on her back. She faces the ceiling with the manuscript inches above her face.

Tricia paces on the other side of the room. "When I left you the pages, I didn't expect you to wait and read them in front of me."

Ava stays focused on the manuscript. "I needed some sleep."

Tricia blows air out of her closed lips, causing them to make a vibrating sound when they flap.

Finally, Ava tosses the manuscript onto the bed, shuts her eyes, and rubs them.

Tricia stares at her until she can't take it anymore. "Well? What's the verdict? I mean, the debate section is a little weak —"

"It's pretty good."

"Excuse me?"

Ava opens her eyes but stares at the ceiling. "You need to cut out about a page of chitchat, but overall, it's a good first act. Not the greatest thing I've ever read, but it doesn't suck."

Tricia is giddy. "It doesn't suck?"

Ava laughs. "Not at all. It reads well. We get a good understanding of the characters. It's a decent opening."

Tricia dives onto the bed and half tackles, half hugs Ava.

"Okay, let's not forget I'm still your hostage."

Tricia relinquishes her bear hug and maneuvers back onto the bed. "You have no idea how much it means to hear those words from you."

"You've come a long way."

Tricia rubs an invisible crease out of her shirt. "I've given it careful consideration, and — I believe in this story. But more than that, I believe in this partnership."

Ava studies her. "It's not a partnership when one person can't leave."

Tricia inches closer to Ava. "But this is bringing out the best in you. A return to the bestseller list. When this manuscript is done, we should move to LA. Together."

"What?"

"We can be roommates. Have late-night writing sessions. Could we use your old agent? Or would we need to get new representation?"

"I'm not moving to LA. I hate that place."

Tricia takes it in stride. "Fine. We can go to New York."

Ava slides away from Tricia. "I'm not living with you. Look here, sweetheart —"

"Don't call me sweetheart!"

Ava freezes.

Tricia closes her eyes. Inhales through the nose. Exhales through the mouth. "It's what my father called me."

"I'm sorry," says Ava.

"I'm all in."

"What do you mean, all in?"

Tricia beams. "I quit my job for this."

Ava pushes herself back into the headboard. It bangs against the wall. "You what?"

"This is my dream. I only have one life. I want to spend it doing something I'm passionate about."

"I'm not doing it, Tricia."

Tricia leaps off the bed and scowls at Ava. "Yes, you are. You have to. This is our dream."

"You sound crazy."

"We are moving to LA or New York, your choice. But we are going, and we will be a writing team. You're going to get back on top and you're taking me with you."

"It's not so easy."

Tricia folds her arms. "You owe me."

Ava studies her. "How could I possibly owe you?"

"I made you what you are. Can't you see it?"

Ava leans forward. "Tricia, what are you talking about?"

"The rumor you claim ruined your life," Tricia smirks. "But made you rich and famous. A gift. From me to you."

Ava's hands shake. "You're lying."

Tricia says, "I did it because you deserve better than this town."

Ava points an accusatory finger at Tricia. "Shut up."

"I only had to tell three people. From there, it spread like wildfire."

Ava swings her legs around to the edge of the bed. "Stop talking."

"By the end of the week, even the teachers knew about it."

Ava leaps to her feet. Points at the door. "Get out!"

Tricia jams her finger in Ava's face. "I made you! You were forged in the fire I lit. Look how you came out."

Ava smacks her finger away. "If you don't get out of here, so help me god."

Tricia makes her way to the door and stops. She turns to Ava and scowls. "You want some dinner?"

Ava bites her lower lip until it reddens with blood as she seethes. "No."

"Fair enough. I'll work on the manuscript. In the meantime, toss the roommate thing around in your head."

Fifteen

Tricia sits at the kitchen table and stares at her laptop. "You're so stupid. Of course, she doesn't want to move back to LA with you. How could you be such an idiot? Fuckin' dumb, dumb, dumb."

She slaps herself. Takes in air through her nose. Slaps herself again. "You're never going to be famous. You're never going to matter."

She slaps herself again. Her cheeks turn red from the abuse.

#

Ava screams into her pillow. It's primal. Desperate.

When it appears she's done, she unleashes another scream.

"Are you okay?" says Tricia.

Ava leaves her head buried in the pillow. "Leave me alone."

Tricia stands in the doorway. She holds a tray with two bottles of water, a sandwich, a bag of chips, and an apple. "I came to clean your bucket."

Ava barks into the pillow. "Go away."

"I also brought some food."

"Leave." The pillow muffles the word.

Tricia says, "I want to apologize. I shouldn't have made all those crazy plans. And I shouldn't have quit my job and expected you to uproot your life for me."

Ava keeps her face buried in the pillow.

Tricia continues, "The best thing I can do is knock this manuscript out as fast as possible so you can read it over and go back to your life."

Ava doesn't respond.

"I'll leave this at the foot of the bed." Tricia sets the tray of food at the foot of the bed, glances into the bucket. "I'll be back to check if this needs to go out in the morning."

Ava screams into her pillow.

In the kitchen, Tricia sits at the table. She's in a zone. Her fingers pound the keys on her laptop.

Ava sits on the floor in the guest bedroom. She stares at the tray of food.

In her office, Tricia stares at the corkboard.

Ava sits on the floor as she nibbles on the sandwich.

Tricia sips a cup of coffee as she paces around the table. Her eyes never leave the laptop screen.

Ava sleeps on the floor in the guest bedroom.

Tricia does yoga in the living room.

The printer spits out page after page of the manuscript.

Morning light from the window spotlights the dolphins on the refrigerator. Tricia blends frozen fruit until it becomes a smoothie. She pours it into two yellow plastic dolphin cups.

Ava lies on the floor, facing away from the door. Her fingers coerce a pencil across a crossword puzzle. There's a knock at the door. "What?"

Tricia enters with a smoothie in each hand, and the manuscript tucked under her arm.

Ava keeps her eyes on the crossword puzzle. "What's a seven-letter synonym for *bitch*?"

Tricia mulls it over, unaware of the insult. "Hellcat?"

Ava keeps her eyes on the crossword. "I'm not going to help you anymore."

Tricia takes a sip from one of the smoothies. "I brought you a smoothie."

"Keep it."

Tricia says, "We've come this far. Might as well see it through." She takes another sip of her smoothie. "Sure, you don't want it? I use honey for a nice hit of sweetness."

"Not interested."

"I've been writing all night. Please read it."

Ava lowers her pencil but still doesn't turn to face Tricia. "After everything you've done to me, you don't understand why I'm not reading your manuscript?"

"Our manuscript. Besides, I apologized."

Ava snorts. "Because you want something from me."

Tricia says, "All I want is your forgiveness."

"And for me to turn you into a writer."

"All I need from you," Tricia says, "is help with an ending. The sooner we're done, the sooner you can leave."

"You've been dangling that carrot since I woke up chained to this bed."

Tricia lets the manuscript fall to the floor. "What do you want to do? Because I will not let you go until we finish this draft."

Ava finally turns to face Tricia. "And all you want is an ending?"

"Correct," Tricia says. "I'll type it and we'll have a first draft. At which point, you'll be free to go."

Ava cracks her knuckles, stands. "Kill yourself."

"What?"

Ava takes a seat at the end of the bed. She keeps her eyes on Tricia the entire time. "Kill yourself. There's your climax."

Tricia asks, "Are you talking about in real life, or in the story?"

"What do you think?"

Tricia takes a moment to mull the question. "Because the book is about us, right now. The things we do, we put in the story."

"I'm aware."

The two women glare at each other.

Finally, Tricia says, "You're serious?"

Ava grins. "It's the dramatic ending the book needs."

Tricia takes a sip of her smoothie. Once again, she offers the other smoothie to Ava.

This time Ava accepts it and takes a sip.

Tricia says, "It's going to be awfully hard for me to have a career as a writer if I'm dead."

Ava takes another sip of her smoothie and lowers the glass. "You'll have something better than a career. You'll have immortality."

"I don't know. Seems so... absolute."

Ava says, "You'll be a pop culture icon."

Tricia stares into her smoothie. "Most people's lives wouldn't even make a mediocre book."

"This would elevate your story." Ava leans in for emphasis. "Make it stand out in a crowd of mediocrity."

"It would show my commitment to the craft."

Ava says, "The ultimate commitment to craft."

Tricia says, "History is full of people who didn't get recognized until after they were dead." She chugs the rest of her smoothie. "This is a big decision. Let me take the rest of the day to mull it over."

Sixteen

The corkboard has two columns. One column reads *Pros*. The other column says *Cons*.

Under the Pros column are notecards with the words:

Fame
Legend
Books
Remembered
TV Specials
Documentary
Pop Culture Icon

Under the Cons column, there is only one solitary card. It reads:

Dead

At the kitchen table, Tricia hand-writes a letter. When she's done, she stuffs it into an envelope and seals it.

Tricia lies on her back under the giant ceramic dolphin in the living room. "Mom, Dad. I'm about to do it. I'm about to prove everyone wrong. I will be somebody. It's not even about having a career as a writer anymore. I'm striving for something much bigger.

When this is done, my name will be remembered for generations. Like Sylvia Plath and Marilyn Monroe. There will be books about me. And documentaries. Maybe even a movie." She pulls herself to her feet and stares straight into the dolphin's eyes. "And the best thing is, I'll be right there with you. God, I can't wait to see the look on your faces."

#

Tricia sets up a tripod inside the guest bedroom. "I gave the suicide idea some thought. It's a stroke of genius, but I've got some feedback."

Ava watches her from the bed. "How full circle of you."

"I know, right?" Tricia sets her phone on top of the tripod. "This is going to play well in the third act. Okay, hear me out. I ran the pros and cons."

"You made a list, didn't you?" says Ava.

"It's an important decision, Ava. Of course I made a list. Now, if I'm going to go through with this, we're going to need a record of it."

Ava says, "You want to film it?"

"Not only are we filming my big moment, but we'll also need to include a video testimonial from each of us."

"There's no way."

Tricia completes the tripod setup and takes a seat at the end of the bed. "You have to. When this is over, the authorities are going to come in here and see me dead in my own house. You'll be the only suspect and we can't have you going to jail, now, can we?"

Ava studies Tricia. "You've covered all the bases, haven't you?"

"I have. During your testimonial, you'll need to look right into the camera and say what happened. You don't have to say it exactly but be sure to say I held you prisoner and there was only one way to escape. You had to use your wits."

Ava shifts and glances at her shaking hands. "Maybe this isn't a good idea."

"It is." Tricia says, "I'll come on and say I'm taking my own life because I owe you. I'll talk about the rumor and how I made your life miserable in high school."

"I take it back. You don't have to do this. It was a joke. Let's not."

Tricia grins. "Ava, can't you see? This is the perfect ending. Eve will use her wits to get out of her situation. And in doing so, not only does she earn her escape, but she gets revenge on the person who ruined her life."

"You didn't ruin my life."

"I didn't make it any easier. And there's the beauty of this. Because in taking my own life, I'm redeemed for what I did. I'm making the ultimate sacrifice."

Ava's eyes fill with tears. She turns her head so Tricia can't see.

Tricia says, "And my final gift for you will be an epic ending to our story. But you'll be the only one left to finish it and reap the rewards." She puts her hand on Ava's knee. "It's so brilliant, you didn't even realize it when you suggested it, did you?"

"I guess not."

Tricia claps, unable to contain her pride. "I wrote a letter to my aunt. She lives in Maine. She's the only family I got left. I'd like for her to get my royalties. She could use the money."

"You sure you want to do this?"

"Absolutely. Remember. After the deed is done, keep the recording. This doesn't work if you go to jail for murdering me. Got it?"

Ava says, "I didn't see you going through with it."

Tricia laughs. "Me either. But more and more, I see this will give me everything I want. And you'll get your comeback. You can move back to LA with your head held high. Bonus points because you get to leave this town behind. Again."

Ava forces a smile.

Tricia says, "Let me do this. After what I did in high school, it's the least I can do."

Ava uses her eyes to tell her *okay*.

Tricia says, "You need a practice run or are you shooting from the hip?"

"I'll shoot from the hip."

Tricia jumps off the bed. "Almost forgot." She sprints out of the bedroom.

The moment she's gone, Ava takes in a huge gulp of air and releases it. She shakes her arms and hands, closes her eyes and takes in another gulp of air and blows it out.

Tricia enters the room and maneuvers around the tripod. She holds a giant kitchen knife. "I'm going to slit my throat. I figured it was the easiest, but also the most dramatic. The most bang for our buck, if you will."

Ava stares at the giant knife.

Tricia says, "You ready?"

"No."

"You better get ready, because it's showtime."

Tricia hits record on the phone and turns to Ava. She motions for Ava to scoot over and look into the camera. Once Ava is in place, Tricia uses her fingers to count backwards.

She holds up three fingers.

She holds up two fingers.

One finger.

She uses it to point to Ava.

Ava stares straight into the camera. "My name is Ava Jordan. I've been held against my will by Tricia Woods. She drugged me, shackled me to a bed, and forced me to write a novel with her. I'm doing this testimonial because... because..." She freezes.

Tricia mouths the phrase *using my wits*.

Ava snaps out of it. "Because, using my wits, I have convinced Tricia to kill herself. This will allow me to escape."

Tricia races over and jumps into the frame right next to Ava. "Hi! I'm Tricia Woods. We're writing a book together, and the ending is going to be my suicide. This serves a multitude of functions. One, it gives Ava the revenge she deserves because I was a bitch to her in high school." Tricia turns to Ava. "Again. Sorry about that."

Inhale through the nose. Exhale through the mouth.

Tricia turns back to the camera. "Two. It gives me a great redemption arc for our story. Three, it shows how clever the main character is, the way she preys on the antagonist's shortcomings in order to earn her escape. It's the perfect ending."

Tricia brings the knife into frame. "Okay. I'm going to slit my throat using this knife." She puts the knife against her throat and stops. "Oh! I almost forgot. I have a letter for my aunt. Please make sure she gets it. Wow! That's everything. Again, so there's no confusion. Ava Jordan did not kill me. I'm the antagonist. Only thing left to say is, I hope you enjoy our book titled *Tina and Eve*."

She turns to Ava. "You like the title?"

Ava wipes a tear off her cheek. "Don't do this."

Tricia turns to the camera and smiles. "This one. So selfless. Be sure to reward her for her valor in the face of adversity." She turns back to Ava, drops a key into her lap, winks, turns back to the camera. "Thanks for watching."

Tricia slits her throat. Blood gushes out of the wound. She collapses out of the frame.

Ava catches her and cradles her as she bleeds out. "Did you start the rumor about me?"

Tricia grins. Exposes a mouth full of blood. "I'm going to be so famous.

Epilogue

Ava, dressed in a stunning rose-colored evening gown, poses in front of a stop-and-repeat. A female reporter rushes to her. She's dressed in a skintight purple dress. She shoves a microphone into Ava's face. "Even before your novel was published, this story has captivated audiences."

Ava chuckles. "It's been one hell of a ride."

The reporter laughs with her. "This is by far the most bizarre adaptation Hollywood has ever seen."

"No argument from me."

The reporter waits to see if Ava will continue. When she doesn't, the reporter continues. "And now, here you are. Back in LA. Attending the premiere of the film based on your novel *Read My Book*. If you could say anything to your former writing partner, Tricia Woods, what would it be?"

Ava turns and glares straight at the camera. "We did it."

THE END

SIGN UP FOR MY AUTHOR NEWSLETTER

Be the first to learn about Eric Williford's new releases and receive exclusive content!

https://thedefpix.com/

Author's Note

I've had these three stories for some time now. I find when you get a seed of an idea, it's in your best interest to take it and run. I've also found these things happen in bunches. The more you create, the more ideas come to you. It all goes hand in hand.

At first, I was going to publish these as standalones. But I watched *The Cabinet of Curiosities*. It reminded me how much I love anthologies. Two of my favorites are the original *Creepshow* and *Tales From The Crypt*.

In my eyes, short stories, collections, and anthologies are the lifeblood of the horror genre. Sometimes you want something you can devour in one or two sittings. Sometimes, you need something to break a reading slump.

Instead of releasing these as stand-alone books, wouldn't it be more fun to package these three stories together and see how readers respond?

Thanks to all my family and friends who have checked out my stories in their various forms. I appreciate your love and support. I love talking to you about crazy films and insane books.

And, of course, thanks to my wife, Allison, who is always there to watch these bizarre movies and shows with me. It may sound crazy, but it's an underrated form of support.

Eric Williford
May 2024
Anaheim, CA

ABOUT THE AUTHOR

Eric Williford grew up in Northern Virginia, where he spent his time playing sports and consuming late-night B movies; he was too young to watch. This love of Roger Corman, Troma, and exploitation films transformed into an award-winning career as an independent filmmaker. *The Big Decay* is his second release.

website: https://thedefpix.com/

www.ingramcontent.com/pod-product-compliance
Lightning Source LLC
Chambersburg PA
CBHW021644260626
47154CB00017BA/2148